ZUCKERMAN UNBOUND

"is masterful, sure in every touch, as clear
and economical of line as a crystal vase...."
—*The New York Times Book Review*

"No one now writing can juggle the somber
and the ludicrous more adroitly than Roth.
...An uncanny sense of pacing and an ear for
dialogue that approaches perfect pitch."
—*Time* magazine

Also by Philip Roth:

THE GHOST WRITER

PHILIP ROTH

Zuckerman Unbound

FAWCETT CREST • NEW YORK

A Fawcett Crest Book
Published by Ballantine Books
Copyright © 1981 by Philip Roth

ISBN 0–449–24521–7

This edition published by arrangement with Farrar,
Straus and Giroux

Selections of this book appeared in somewhat different
form in *The Atlantic*, *The New Yorker*, and *Playboy*.

Manufactured in the United States of America

First Ballantine Books Edition: July 1982
10 9 8 7 6 5 4 3 2 1

For PHILIP GUSTON
1913–1980

"Let Nathan see what it is to be lifted from obscurity. Let him not come hammering at our door to tell us that he wasn't warned."

E. I. LONOFF
to his wife
December 10, 1956

Zuckerman Unbound

"I'm Alvin Pepler"

What the hell are you doing on a bus, with your dough?"

It was a small, husky young fellow with a short haircut and a new business suit who wanted to know; he had been daydreaming over an automotive magazine until he saw who was sitting next to him. That was all it took to charge him up.

Undaunted by Zuckerman's unobliging reply—on a bus to be transported through space—he happily offered his advice. These days everybody did, if they could find him. "You should buy a helicopter. That's how I'd do it. Rent the landing rights up on apartment buildings and fly straight over the dog-poop. Hey, see this guy?" This second question was for a man standing in the aisle reading his *Times*.

The bus was traveling south on Fifth Avenue, downtown from Zuckerman's new Upper East Side address. He was off to see an investment specialist on Fifty-second Street, a meeting arranged by his agent, André Schevitz, to get him to diversify his capital. Gone were the days when Zuckerman had only to worry about Zuckerman making money: henceforth he would have to worry about his money making money. "Where do you have it right now?" the investment specialist had asked when Zuckerman finally phoned. "In my shoe," Zuckerman told him. The investment specialist laughed. "You intend to keep it there?" Though the answer was yes, it was easier for the moment to say no. Zuckerman had privately declared a one-year moratorium on all serious decisions arising out of the smashing success. When he could think straight again, he would act again. All this, this luck—what did it mean? Coming so suddenly, and on such a scale, it was as baffling as a misfortune.

Because Zuckerman was not ordinarily going anywhere at the morning rush hour—except into his study with his coffee cup to

reread the paragraphs from the day before—
he hadn't realized until too late that it was
a bad time to be taking a bus. But then he
still refused to believe that he was any less
free than he'd been six weeks before to come
and go as he liked, when he liked, without
having to remember beforehand who he was.
Ordinary everyday thoughts on the subject
of who one was were lavish enough without
an extra hump of narcissism to carry around.

"Hey. *Hey*." Zuckerman's excited neighbor
was trying again to distract the man in the
aisle from his *Times*. "See this guy next to
me?"

"I do now," came the stern, affronted reply.

"He's the guy who wrote *Carnovsky*. Didn't
you read about it in the papers? He just made
a million bucks and he's taking a bus."

Upon hearing that a millionaire was on
board, two girls in identical gray uniforms—
two frail, sweet-looking children, undoubtedly well-bred little sisters on their way
downtown to convent school—turned to look
at him.

"Veronica," said the smaller of the two, "it's
the man who wrote the book that Mummy's
reading. It's Carnovsky."

The children kneeled on their seats so as

to face him. A middle-aged couple in the row across from the children also turned to get a look.

"Go on, girls," said Zuckerman lightly. "Back to your homework."

"Our mother," said the older child, taking charge, "is reading your book, Mr. Carnovsky."

"Fine. But Mummy wouldn't want you to stare on the bus."

No luck. Must be phrenology they were studying at St. Mary's.

Zuckerman's companion had meanwhile turned to the seat directly behind to explain to the woman there the big goings-on. Make her a part of it. The family of man. "I'm sitting next to a guy who just made a million bucks. Probably two."

"Well," said a gentle, ladylike voice, "I hope all that money doesn't change him."

Fifteen blocks north of the investment specialist's office, Zuckerman pulled the cord and got off. Surely here, in the garden spot of anomie, it was still possible to be nobody on the rush-hour streets. If not, try a mustache. This may be far from life as you feel, see, know, and wish to know it, but if all it takes is a mustache, then, for Christ's sake, grow one.

14

You are not Paul Newman, but you're no longer who you used to be either. A mustache. Contact lenses. Maybe a colorful costume would help. Try looking the way everybody does today instead of the way everybody looked twenty years ago in Humanities 2. Less like Albert Einstein, more like Jimi Hendrix, and you won't stick out so much. And what about your gait while you're at it? He was always meaning to work on that anyway. Zuckerman moved with his knees too close together and at a much too hurried pace. A man six feet tall should *amble* more. But he could never remember about ambling after the first dozen steps—twenty, thirty paces and he was lost in his thoughts instead of thinking about his stride. Well, now was the time to get on with it, especially with his sex credentials coming under scrutiny in the press. As aggressive in the walk as in the work. You're a millionaire, walk like one. People are watching.

The joke was on him. Someone was—the woman who'd had to be told on the bus why everyone else was agog. A tall, thin, elderly woman, her face heavily powdered...only why was she running after him? And undoing

15

the latch on her purse? Suddenly his adrenalin advised Zuckerman to run too.

You see, not everybody was delighted by this book that was making Zuckerman a fortune. Plenty of people had already written to tell him off. "For depicting Jews in a peepshow atmosphere of total perversion, for depicting Jews in acts of adultery, exhibitionism, masturbation, sodomy, fetishism, and whoremongery," somebody with letterhead stationery as impressive as the President's had even suggested that he "ought to be shot." And in the spring of 1969 this was no longer just an expression. Vietnam was a slaughterhouse, and off the battlefield as well as on, many Americans had gone berserk. Just about a year before, Martin Luther King and Robert Kennedy had been gunned down by assassins. Closer to home, a former teacher of Zuckerman's was still hiding out because a rifle had been fired at him through his kitchen window as he'd been sitting at his table one night with a glass of warm milk and a Wodehouse novel. The retired bachelor had taught Middle English at the University of Chicago for thirty-five years. The course had been hard, though not that hard. But a bloody nose wasn't enough anymore. Blowing people apart seemed to have replaced the roundhouse punch in the daydreams of the aggrieved: only annihilation gave satisfaction that lasted. At the Democratic convention the summer before, hundreds had been beaten with clubs and trampled by horses and thrown through plate-glass windows for offenses against order and decency less grave than Zuckerman's were thought to be by any number of his correspondents. It didn't strike Zuckerman as at all unlikely that in a seedy room somewhere the *Life* cover featuring his face (unmustached) had been tacked up within dart-throwing distance of the bed of some "loner." Those cover stories were enough of a trial for a writer's writer friends, let alone for a semi-literate psychopath who might not know about all the good deeds he did at the PEN Club. Oh, Madam, if only you knew the real me! Don't shoot! I am a serious writer as well as one of the boys!

But it was too late to plead his cause. Behind her rimless spectacles, the powdered zealot's pale green eyes were glazed with conviction; at point-blank range she had hold of his arm. "Don't"—she was not young, and it was a struggle for her to catch her breath— "don't let all that money change you, whoever

17

you may be. Money never made anybody
happy. Only He can do that." And from her
Luger-sized purse she removed a picture post-
card of Jesus and pressed it into his hand.
"'There is not a just man upon earth,'" she
reminded him, "'that doeth good and sinneth
not. If we say that we have no sin, we deceive
ourselves, and the truth is not in us.'"

He was sipping coffee later that morning at
a counter around the corner from the office
of the investment specialist—studying, for
the first time in his life, the business page of
the morning paper—when a smiling middle-
aged woman came up to tell him that from
reading about his sexual liberation in *Carnovsky,* she was less "uptight" now herself.
In the bank at Rockefeller Plaza where he
went to cash a check, the long-haired guard
asked in a whisper if he could touch Mr. Zuckerman's coat: he wanted to tell his wife about
it when he got home that night. While he was
walking through the park, a nicely dressed
young East Side mother out with her baby
and her dog stepped into his path and said,
"You need love, and you need it all the time.
I feel sorry for you." In the periodical room

of the Public Library an elderly gentleman tapped him on the shoulder and in heavily accented English—Zuckerman's grandfather's English—told him how sorry he felt for his parents. "You didn't put in your whole life," he said sadly. "There's much more to your life than that. But you just leave it out. To get even." And then, at last, at home, a large jovial black man from Con Ed who was waiting in the hall to read his meter. "Hey, you do all that stuff in that book? With all those chicks? You are something else, man." The meter reader. But people didn't just read meters anymore, they also read that book.

Zuckerman was tall, but not as tall as Wilt Chamberlain. He was thin, but not as thin as Mahatma Gandhi. In his customary getup of tan corduroy coat, gray turtleneck sweater, and cotton khaki trousers he was neatly attired, but hardly Rubirosa. Nor was dark hair and a prominent nose the distinguishing mark in New York that it would have been in Reykjavik or Helsinki. But two, three, four times a week, they spotted him anyway. "It's Carnovsky!" "Hey, careful, Carnovsky, they arrest people for that!" "Hey, want to see my underwear, Gil?" In the beginning, when he heard someone call after him out on the

street, he would wave hello to show what a
good sport he was. It was the easiest thing to
do, so he did it. Then the easiest thing was
to pretend not to hear and keep going. Then
the easiest thing was to pretend that he was
hearing things, to realize that it was happening in a world that didn't exist. They had
mistaken impersonation for confession and
were calling out to a character who lived in
a book. Zuckerman tried taking it as praise—
he had made real people believe Carnovsky
real too—but in the end he pretended he was
only himself, and with his quick, small steps
hurried on.

At the end of the day he walked out of his
new neighborhood and over to Yorkville, and
on Second Avenue found the haven he was
looking for. Just the place to be left to himself
with the evening paper, or so he thought
when he peered between the salamis strung
up in the window: a sixty-year-old waitress
in runny eye shadow and crumbling house
slippers, and behind the sandwich counter,
wearing an apron about as fresh as a Manhattan snowdrift, a colossus with a carving

knife. It was a few minutes after six. He could grab a sandwich and be off the streets by seven.

"Pardon me."

Zuckerman looked up from the fraying menu at a man in a dark raincoat who was standing beside his table. The dozen or so other tables were empty. The stranger was carrying a hat in his hands in a way that restored to that expression its original metaphorical luster.

"Pardon me. I only want to say thank you."

He was a large man, chesty, with big sloping shoulders and a heavy neck. A single strand of hair looped over his bald head, but otherwise his face was a boy's: shining smooth cheeks, emotional brown eyes, an impudent owlish little beak.

"Thank me? For what?" The first time in the six weeks that it had occurred to Zuckerman to pretend that he was another person entirely. He was learning.

His admirer took it for humility. The lively, lachrymose eyes deepened with feeling. "God! For everything. The humor. The compassion. The understanding of our deepest drives. For all you have reminded us about the human comedy."

Compassion? Understanding? Only hours earlier the old man in the library had told him how sorry he felt for his family. They had him coming and going today.

"Well," said Zuckerman, "that's very kind."

The stranger pointed to the menu in Zuckerman's hand. "Please, order. I didn't mean to obtrude. I was in the washroom, and when I came out I couldn't believe my eyes. To see you in a place like this. I just had to come up and say thanks before I left."

"Quite all right."

"What makes it unbelievable is that I'm a Newarker myself."

"Are you?"

"Born and bred. You got out in forty-nine, right? Well, it's a different city today. You wouldn't recognize it. You wouldn't want to."

"So I hear."

"Me, I'm still over there, pounding away."

Zuckerman nodded, and signaled for the waitress.

"I don't think people can appreciate what you're doing for the old Newark unless they're from there themselves."

Zuckerman ordered his sandwich and some tea. How does he know I left in forty-nine? I suppose from *Life*.

He smiled and waited for the fellow to be on his way back across the river.

"You're our Marcel Proust, Mr. Zuckerman."

Zuckerman laughed. It wasn't exactly how he saw it.

"I mean it. It's not a put-on. God forbid. In my estimation you are up there with Stephen Crane. You are the two great Newark writers."

"Well, that's kind of you."

"There's Mary Mapes Dodge, but however much you may admire *Hans Brinker,* it's still only a book for children. I would have to place her third. Then there is LeRoi Jones, but him I have no trouble placing fourth. I say this without racial prejudice, and not as a result of the tragedy that has happened to the city in recent years, but what he writes is not literature. In my estimation it is black propaganda. No, in literature we have got you and Stephen Crane, in acting we have got Rod Steiger and Vivian Blaine, in playwrighting we have got Dore Schary, in singing we have got Sarah Vaughan, and in sports we have got Gene Hermanski and Herb Krautblatt. Not that you can mention sports and what you have accomplished in the same breath.

In years to come I honestly see schoolchildren visiting the city of Newark—"

"Oh," said Zuckerman, amused again, but uncertain as to what might be feeding such effusiveness, "oh, I think it's going to take more than me to bring the schoolchildren in. Especially with the Empire shut down." The Empire was the Washington Street burlesque house, long defunct, where many a New Jersey boy had in the half light seen his first G-string. Zuckerman was one, Gilbert Carnovsky another.

The fellow raised his arms—and his hat: gesture of helpless surrender. "Well, you have got the great sense of humor in life too. No comeback from me could equal that. But you'll see. It'll be you they turn to in the future when they want to remember what it was like in the old days. In *Carnovsky* you have pinned down for all time growing up in that town as a Jew."

"Well, thanks again. Thank you, really, for all the kind remarks."

The waitress appeared with his sandwich. That should end it. On a pleasant note, actually. Behind the effusiveness lay nothing but somebody who had enjoyed a book. Fine. "Thank you," said Zuckerman—the fourth time—and ceremoniously lifted half of his sandwich.

"I went to South Side. Class of forty-three."

South Side High, at the decaying heart of the old industrial city, had been almost half black even in Zuckerman's day, when Newark was still mostly white. His own school district, at the far edge of a newer residential Newark, had been populated in the twenties and thirties by Jews leaving the rundown immigrant enclaves in the central wards to rear children bound for college and the professions and, in time, for the Orange suburbs, where Zuckerman's own brother, Henry, now owned a big house.

"You're Weequahic forty-nine."

"Look," said Zuckerman apologetically, "I have to eat and run. I'm sorry."

"Forgive me, please. I only wanted to say—well, I said it, didn't I?" He smiled regretfully at his own insistence. "Thank you, thank you again. For everything. It's been a pleasure. It's been a thrill. I didn't mean to bug you, God knows."

Zuckerman watched him move off to the register to pay for his meal. Younger than he seemed from the dark clothes and the beefy build and the vanquished air, but more ungainly, and, with his heavy splayfooted walk, more pathetic than Zuckerman had realized.

"Excuse me. I'm sorry."

Hat in hand again. Zuckerman was sure he had seen him go out the door with it on his head.

"Yes?"

"This is probably going to make you laugh. But I'm trying to write myself. You don't have to worry about the competition, I assure you. When you try your hand at it, then you really admire the stupendous accomplishment of somebody like yourself. The patience alone is phenomenal. Day in and day out facing that white piece of paper."

Zuckerman had been thinking that he should have had the good grace to ask him to sit and chat, if only for a moment. He had even begun to feel a sentimental connection, remembering him standing beside the table, announcing, "I'm a Newarker myself." He was feeling less sentimental with the Newarker standing back beside the table announcing that he was a writer too.

"I was wondering if you could recommend an editor or an agent who might be able to help someone like me."

"No."

"Okay. Fine. No problem. Just asking. I already have a producer, you see, who wants to make a musical out of my life. My own feeling is that it should come out first in public as a serious book. With all the facts."

Silence.

"That sounds preposterous to you, I know, even if you're too polite to say so. But it's true. It has nothing to do with me being anybody who matters. I ain't and I don't. One look and you know that. It's what happened to me that'll make the musical."

Silence.

"I'm Alvin Pepler."

Well, he wasn't Houdini. For a moment that had seemed in the cards.

Alvin Pepler waited to hear what Nathan Zuckerman made of meeting Alvin Pepler. When he heard nothing, he quickly came to Zuckerman's aid. And his own. "Of course to people like you the name can't mean a thing. You have better things to do with your time than waste it on TV. But I thought, as we're *landsmen,* that maybe your family might have mentioned me to you. I didn't say this earlier, I didn't think it was in order, but your father's cousin, Essie Slifer, happened to go to Central with my mother's sister Lottie way

27

back when. They were one year apart. I don't know if this helps, but I'm the one they called in the papers 'Pepler the Man of the People.' I'm 'Alvin the Jewish Marine.'"

"Why then," said Zuckerman, relieved at last to have something to say, "you're the quiz contestant, no? You were on one of those shows."

Oh, there was more to it than that. The syrupy brown eyes went mournful and angry, filling up not with tears, but what was worse, with *truth*. "Mr. Zuckerman, for three consecutive weeks I was the winner on the biggest of them all. Bigger than 'Twenty-One.' In terms of dollars given away bigger than 'The $64,000 Question.' I was the winner on 'Smart Money.'"

Zuckerman couldn't remember ever seeing any of those quiz shows back in the late fifties, and didn't know one from another; he and his first wife, Betsy, hadn't even owned a television set. Still, he thought he could remember somebody in his family—more than likely Cousin Essie—once mentioning a Pepler family from Newark, and their oddball son, the quiz contestant and ex-Marine.

"It was Alvin Pepler they cut down to make way for the great Hewlett Lincoln. That is the subject of my book. The fraud perpetrated on the American public. The manipulation of the trust of tens of millions of innocent people. And how for admitting it I have been turned into a pariah until this day. They made me and then they destroyed me, and, Mr. Zuckerman, they haven't finished with me yet. The others involved have all gone on, onward and upward in corporate America, and nobody cares a good goddamn what thieves and liars they were. But because I wouldn't lie for those miserable crooks, I have spent ten years as a marked man. A McCarthy victim is better off than I am. The whole country rose up against that bastard, and vindicated the innocent and so on, till at least some justice was restored. But Alvin Pepler, to this day, is a dirty name throughout the American broadcasting industry."

Zuckerman was remembering more clearly now the stir those quiz shows had made, remembering not so much Pepler but Hewlett Lincoln, the philosophical young country newspaperman and son of the Republican governor of Maine, and, while he was a contestant, the most famous television celebrity in America, admired by schoolchildren, their teachers, their parents, their grandparents—

until the scandal broke, and the schoolchildren learned that the answers that came trippingly off the tongue of Hewlett Lincoln in the contestants' isolation booth had been slipped to him days earlier by the show's producers. There were front-page stories in the papers, and as Zuckerman recalled, the ludicrous finale had been a Congressional investigation.

"I wouldn't dream," Pepler was saying, "of comparing the two of us. An educated artist like yourself and a person who happens to be born with a photographic memory are two different things entirely. But while I was on 'Smart Money,' deservedly or not I had the respect of the entire nation. If I have to say so myself, I don't think it did the Jewish people any harm having a Marine veteran of two wars representing them on prime-time national television for three consecutive weeks. You may have contempt for quiz programs, even the honest ones. You have a right to— you more than anybody. But the average person didn't see it that way in those days. That's why when I was on top for those three great weeks, I made no bones about my religion. I said it right out. I wanted the country to know that a Jew in the Marine Corps could be as tough on the battlefield as anyone. I never claimed I was a war hero. Far from it. I shook like the next guy in a foxhole, but I never ran, even under fire. Of course there were a lot of Jews in combat, and braver men than me. But I was the one who got that point across to the great mass of the American people, and if I did it by way of a quiz show— well, that was the way that was given to me. Then, of course, *Variety* started calling me names, calling me 'quizling' and so on, and that was the beginning of the end. Quizling, with a *z*. When I was the only one who didn't want their answers to begin with! When all I wanted was for them to give me the subject, to let me study and memorize, and then to fight it out fair and square! I could fill volumes about those people and what they did to me. That's why running into you, coming upon Newark's great writer out of the blue— well, it strikes me as practically a miracle at this point in my life. Because if I could write a publishable book, I honestly think that people would read it and that they would believe it. My name would be restored to what it was. That little bit of good I did would not be wiped away forever, as it is now. Whoever innocent I harmed and left besmirched, all the millions

I let down, Jews particularly—well, they would finally understand the truth of what happened. They would forgive me."

His own aria had not left him unmoved. The deep brown irises were cups of ore fresh from the furnace—as though a drop of Pepler's eyes could burn a hole right through you.

"Well, if that's the case," said Zuckerman, "you should work at it."

"I have." Pepler smiled the best he could. "Ten years of my life. May I?" He pointed to the empty chair across the table.

"Why not?" said Zuckerman, and tried not to think of all the reasons.

"I've worked at nothing else," said Pepler, plunging excitedly onto the seat. "I've worked at nothing else every night *for ten years*. But I don't have the gift. That's what they tell me anyway. I have sent my book to twenty-two publishers. I have rewritten it five times. I pay a young teacher from Columbia High in South Orange, which is still an A-rated school—I pay her by the hour to correct my grammar and punctuation wherever it's wrong. I wouldn't dream of submitting a single page of this book without her going over it beforehand for my errors. It's all too important for that. But if in their estimation you don't have the great gift—well, that's it. You may chalk this up to bitterness. I would too, in your shoes. But Miss Diamond, this teacher working with me, she agrees: by now all they have to see is that Alvin Pepler is the author and they throw it in the pile marked trash. I don't think they read past my name. By now I'm one big laugh, even to the lowliest editor on Publishers' Row." The speech was fervent, yet the gaze, now that he was at the level of the table, seemed drawn to what was uneaten on Zuckerman's plate. "That's why I asked you about an agent, an editor—somebody fresh who wouldn't be prejudiced right off. Who would understand that this is *serious*."

Zuckerman, sucker though he was for seriousness, was still not going to be drawn into a discussion about agents and editors. If ever there was a reason for an American writer to seek asylum in Red China, it would be to put ten thousand miles between himself and those discussions.

"There's still the musical," Zuckerman reminded him.

"A serious book is one thing, and a Broadway musical is something else."

Another discussion Zuckerman would as

soon avoid. Sounded like the premise for a course at the New School.

"If," said Pepler weakly, "it even gets made."

Optimistic Zuckerman: "Well, if you've got a producer..."

"Yes, but so far it's only a gentlemen's agreement. No money has changed hands, nobody's signed anything. The work is supposed to start when he gets back. That's when we make the real deal."

"Well, *that's* something."

"It's why I'm in New York. I'm living over at his place, talking into a tape machine. That's all I'm supposed to do. He doesn't want to read what I wrote any more than the moguls on Publishers' Row. Just talk into the machine till he gets back. And leave out the thoughts. Just the stories. Well, beggars can't be choosers."

As good a note as any to leave on.

"But," said Pepler, when he saw Zuckerman get to his feet, "but you've eaten only half a sandwich!"

"Can't." He indicated the hour on his watch. "Someone waiting. Meeting."

"Oh, forgive me, Mr. Zuckerman, I'm sorry."

"Good luck with the musical." He reached

down and shook Pepler's hand. "Good luck all around." Pepler was unable to hide the disappointment. Pepler was unable to hide *anything*. Or was that hiding everything? Impossible to tell, and another reason to go.

"Thanks a million." Then, with resignation, "Look, to switch from the sublime..."

What now?

"You don't mind, do you, if I eat your pickle?"

Was this a joke? Was this satire?

"I can't stay away from this stuff," he explained. "Childhood hang-up."

"Please," said Zuckerman, "go right ahead."

"Sure you don't—?"

"No, no."

He was also eyeing the uneaten half of Zuckerman's sandwich. And it was no joke. Too driven for that. "While I'm at it—" he said, with a self-deprecating smile.

"Sure, why not."

"See, there's no food in their refrigerator. I talk into that tape machine with all those stories and I get starved. I wake up in the night with something I forgot for the machine, and there's nothing to eat." He began wrapping the half sandwich in a napkin from

35

the dispenser on the table. "Everything is send-out."

But Zuckerman was well on his way. At the register he put down a five and kept going.

Pepler popped up two blocks to the west, while Zuckerman waited for a light on Lexington. "One last thing—"

"Look—"

"Don't worry," said Pepler, "I'm not going to ask you to read my book. Nuts I am"—the admission registered in Zuckerman's chest with a light thud—"but not that nuts. You don't ask Einstein to check your bank statements."

The novelist's apprehension was hardly mitigated by the flattery. "Mr. Pepler, what do you want from me?"

"I just wonder if you think this project is right for a producer like Marty Paté. Because that's who's after it. I didn't want to bandy names around, but, okay, that's who it is. My worry isn't even the money. I don't intend to get screwed—not again—but the hell with the money for now. What I'm wondering to myself is if I can trust him to do justice to my life, to what I have been put through in this country *all my life*."

Scorn, betrayal, humiliation—the eyes disclosed for Zuckerman everything Pepler had been put through, and without "thoughts."

Zuckerman looked for a taxi. "Couldn't say."

"But you know Paté."

"Never heard of him."

"Marty Paté. The Broadway producer."

"Nope."

"But—" He looked like some large animal just batted on the head at the abattoir, badly stunned but not quite out. He looked in agony. "But—he knows *you*. He met you— through Miss O'Shea. When you were all in Ireland. For her birthday."

According to the columnists, the movie star Caesara O'Shea and the novelist Nathan Zuckerman were an "item." Actually, off the screen, Zuckerman had met with her but once in his life, as her dinner partner at the Schevitzes' some ten days before.

"Hey, how is Miss O'Shea, by the way? I wish," said Pepler, now suddenly wistful, "I could tell her—I wish you could tell her *for* me—what a great lady she is. To the public. To my mind she is the only real lady left in the movies today. Nothing they say could besmirch Miss O'Shea. I mean that."

37

"I'll tell her." The easiest way. Short of running for it.

"I stayed up Tuesday to watch her—she was on the Late Show. *Divine Mission.* Another incredible coincidence. Watching that and then meeting you. I watched with Paté's father. You remember Marty's old man? From Ireland? Mr. Perlmutter?"

"Vaguely." Why not, if it brought this fellow's fever down?

By now the light had changed several times. When Zuckerman crossed, Pepler did too.

"He lives with Paté. In the town house. You ought to get a load of the layout over there," Pepler said. "Offices downstairs on the main floor. Autographed photos all along the hallway coming in. You should see of who. Victor Hugo, Sarah Bernhardt, Enrico Caruso. Marty has a dealer who gets them for him. Names like that, and by the yard. There's a fourteen-carat chandelier, there's an oil painting of Napoleon, there's velvet drapes right to the floor. And this is only the office. There's a harp in the hallway, just sitting there. Mr. Perlmutter says Marty directed all the decoration himself. From pictures of Versailles. He has a valuable collection from the Napo-

leonic era. The drinking glasses even have
gold rims, like Napoleon had. Then upstairs,
where Marty actually lives, resides, completely done up in modern design. Red leather,
recessed lights, pitch-black walls. Plants like
in an oasis. You should see the bathroom. Cut
flowers *in the bathroom*. The floral bill is a
thousand a month. Toilets like dolphins and
the handles on everything gold-plate. And the
food is all send-out, down to salt and pepper.
Nobody prepares anything. Nobody washes
a dish. He's got a million-dollar kitchen in
there and I don't think anybody's ever used
it except to get water for an aspirin. A line
on the phone direct to the restaurant next
door. The old man calls down and the next
thing, shish kebab. In flames. You know who
else is living there right now? Of course she
comes and she goes, but she was the one who
let me in with my suitcase when I got here
Monday. She showed me to my room. She
found me my towels. Gayle Gibraltar."

The name meant nothing to Zuckerman.
All he could think was that if he kept walking, he was going to have Pepler with him all
the way home, and if he hailed a cab, Pepler
would hop in.

"I wouldn't want to take you out of your way," Zuckerman said.

"No problem. Paté's on Sixty-second and Madison. We're almost neighbors."

How did he know that?

"You're a very approachable guy, really, aren't you? I was terrified even to come up to you. My heart was pounding. I didn't think I had the nerve. I read in the *Star-Ledger* where fans bugged you so much you went around in a limousine with drawn shutters and two gorillas for bodyguards." The *Star-Ledger* was Newark's morning paper.

"That's Sinatra."

Pepler enjoyed that one. "Well, it's like the critics say, nobody can top you with the one-liner. Of course, Sinatra's from Jersey too. Hoboken's own. He still comes back to see his mother. People don't realize how many of us there are."

"Us?"

"Boys from Jersey who became household words. You wouldn't be offended, would you, if I eat the sandwich now? It can get pretty greasy carrying around."

"Suit yourself."

"I don't want to embarrass you. The hick

from home. This is your town, and you being you—"

"Mr. Pepler, it means nothing to me either way."

Gently undoing the paper napkin like a surgical dressing, leaning forward so as not to soil himself, Pepler prepared for the first bite. "I shouldn't eat this stuff," he told Zuckerman. "Not anymore. In the service I was the guy who could eat anything. I was a joke. Pepler the human garbage can. I was famous for it. Under fire in Korea I survived on stuff you wouldn't feed a dog. Washed down with snow. You wouldn't believe what I had to eat. But then those bastards made me lose to Lincoln on only my third week—a three-part question on Americana I could have answered in my sleep—and my stomach trouble dates from that night. *All* my trouble dates from that night. That's a fact. That was the night that did me in. I can document it with doctors' reports. It's all in the book." That said, he bit into the sandwich. A quick second bite. A third. Gone. No sense prolonging the agony.

Zuckerman offered his handkerchief.

"Thanks," said Pepler. "My God, look at me, wiping my mouth with Nathan Zuckerman's hankie."

Zuckerman raised a hand to indicate that he should take it in stride. Pepler laughed uproariously.

"But," he said, carefully cleaning his fingers, "getting back to Paté, what you're saying, Nathan—"

Nathan.

"—is that by and large I shouldn't have much worry with a producer of his caliber, and the kind of outfit he runs."

"I didn't say anything of the sort."

"But"—alarmed! again the abattoir!—"you know him, you met him in Ireland. You said so!"

"Briefly."

"Ah, but that's how Marty meets everybody. He wouldn't get everything in otherwise. The phone rings and you hear the secretary over the intercom telling the old man to pick up, and you can't believe your ears."

"Victor Hugo on the line."

Pepler's laughter was uncontrollable. "Not far from it, Nathan." He was having an awfully good time now. And, Zuckerman had to admit it, so was he. Once you relaxed with this guy, he wasn't unentertaining. You could pick up worse on the way home from the delicatessen.

Except how does he know we're almost neighbors? And how do you shake him off?

"It's a Who's Who of International Entertainment, the calls coming into that place. I tell you what gives me the greatest faith in this project getting off the ground, and that's where Marty happens to be right now. On business. Take a guess."

"No idea."

"Take a guess. You especially will be impressed."

"I especially."

"Absolutely."

"You've got me, Alvin." Alvin.

"Israel," announced Pepler. "With Moshe Dayan."

"Well, well."

"He's got an option on the Six-Day War, for a musical. Yul Brynner is already as good as signed to star as Dayan. With Brynner it could be something for the Jews."

"And for Paté, too, no?"

"Christ, how can he miss? He'll rake it in. They're all but sold out the first year on theater parties alone. This is without even a script. Mr. Perlmutter has sounded them out.

They're ecstatic from just the idea. I tell you something else. Highly classified. When he gets back next week from Israel, I wouldn't be surprised if he approaches Nathan Zuckerman to do the adaptation of the war for the stage."

"They're thinking of me."

"You, Herman Wouk, and Harold Pinter. Those are the three names they're kicking around."

"Mr. Pepler."

"'Alvin' is fine."

"Alvin, who told you all this?"

"Gayle. Gibraltar."

"How does she come by such classified information?"

"Oh, well, God. For one thing, she's a terrific business brain. People don't realize, because the beauty is all they see. But before she became a Playmate, she used to work as a guide at the United Nations. She speaks four languages. It was Playmate of the Month that launched her, of course."

"Into?"

"You name it. She and Paté literally don't stop. Those two are the secret of perpetual motion. Marty found out before he left that it was Dayan's son's birthday and so Gayle went out and got him a present: a solid-chocolate chess set. And the boy loved it. Last night she went up to Massachusetts to jump from an airplane today for UNESCO. It was a benefit. And in the Sardinian film they just finished, she did her own stunts on the horse."

"So she's an actress too. In Sardinian films."

"Well, it was a Sardinian corporation. The film was international. Look"—suddenly shyness overcame him—"she's not Miss O'Shea, not by a long shot. Miss O'Shea has style. Miss O'Shea has class. Gayle is somebody...without hang-ups. That's what she projects, you see. When you're with her."

Pepler turned a bright red speaking about what was projected by Gayle Gibraltar when you were with her.

"Which are her four languages?" asked Zuckerman.

"I'm not sure. English, of course, is one. I haven't had a chance to check out the others."

"I would, in your shoes."

"Well, okay, I will. Good idea. Latvian must be another. That's where she was born."

"And Paté's father. Which four languages does he speak?"

Pepler saw he was being needled. But then,

45

not by just anybody; he took it, after a moment, with another hearty, appreciative laugh. "Oh, don't worry. It's all straight from the shoulder with that guy. You couldn't meet a finer old-timer. Shakes your hand whenever you come in. Beautifully turned out, but in a sedate manner, always. Always with this nice, respectful, soft-spoken air. No, the one who gives me the confidence, frankly, is this lovely, dignified old gentleman. He keeps the books, he signs the checks, and when the decisions are made, I tell you, in his own quiet, respectful way, he makes them. He hasn't got Marty's go-go razzle-dazzle, but this is the rock, the foundation."

"I hope so."

"Please, don't worry about me. I learned my lesson. They wiped me out worse than you can begin to imagine back when they wiped me out. I haven't been the same person since. I start back after the war, and then there's Korea. I start back again after that, fight my way to the absolute top, and whammo. This actually is the best week I have had in ten years, being here in New York City with finally, *finally*, some kind of door to the future opening up. My good name, my robust health, my Marine record, and then my lovely, loyal

46

fiancée, who took to the hills. I never saw her again. I became a walking disgrace because of those crooked bastards, and I'm not about to lay myself open like that ever again. I understand what you're trying to warn me about in your own humorous way. Well, don't worry, the one-liners aren't wasted on me. I'm warned. I'm not the wide-eyed little yokel I was back in fifty-nine. I don't think I'm with a great man anymore just because a guy has got a hundred pair of shoes in the closet and a Jacuzzi bathtub ten feet long. They were going to make me a sportscaster on the Sunday night news, did you know that? I was supposed to be Stan Lomax by now. I was supposed to be Bill Stern."

"But they didn't do it," said Zuckerman.

"May I speak frankly, Nathan? I would give anything to sit down with you for one evening, any night you wanted, and tell you what was going on in this country in the reign of Ike the Great. In my opinion the beginning of the end of what's good in this country were those quiz shows and the crooks that ran them and the public that swallowed it like so many dopes. There is where it began, and where it has ended is with another war again, and one this time that makes you want to scream. And a liar like Nixon as President of the United States. Eisenhower's gift to America. That schmegeggy in his golf shoes—this is what he leaves for posterity. But this is all in my book, spelled out in detail, step by step, the decline of every decent American thing into liars and lies. You can well understand why I have my own reasons for being nervous about throwing my lot in with anybody, Marty Paté included. After all, mine is not the kind of criticism of a country that you are used to finding in a Broadway musical. Do you agree? Can such a thing even be made into a musical without watering down the condemnation I make of the system?"

"I don't know."

"They promised me a job as a sportscaster if I didn't admit to the D.A. about how the thing was rigged from the day it started, how even that little girl they had on, age eleven and in pigtails, they gave her the answers and didn't even tell her mother. They were going to put me on TV every Sunday night with the sports results. It was all arranged. So they told me. 'Al Pepler and the Weekend Round-up.' And from there to broadcasting the Yankee home games. What it came down to was that they couldn't afford to let a Jew be a big winner too long on 'Smart Money.' Especially a Jew who made no bones about it. They were afraid about the ratings. They were terrified they would rub the country the wrong way. Bateman and Schachtman, the producers, would have meetings about things like this and talk about it together till all hours. They would talk about whether to have an armed guard come on the stage with the questions, or the president of a bank. They would talk about whether the isolation booth should be waiting on the stage at the beginning or whether it should be rolled out by a squad of Eagle Scouts. They would talk all night long, two grown men, about what kind of tie I should wear. This is all true, Nathan. But my point is that if you study the programs the way I have, you'll see that my theory about the Jews is borne out. There were twenty quiz shows on three networks, seven of them in action five days a week. On an average week they gave away half a million bucks. I'm talking about true quiz shows, exclusive of panel shows and stunt shows and those do-good shows, where you could only get on if you had palsy or no feet. Half a million bucks a week, and yet over the bonanza period from nineteen fifty-five to fifty-eight, you won't find a single Jew who won over a hundred thousand. That was the limit for a Jew to win, and this is on programs where the producers, nearly every single one, were Jews themselves. To break the bank you had to be a goy like Hewlett. The bigger the goy, the bigger the haul. This is on programs *run* by Jews. This is what still drives me crazy. 'I will study and get ready, and maybe the chance will come.' You know who said that? Abraham Lincoln. The real Lincoln. That was who I quoted from on nationwide TV my first night on the show; before I got into the booth. Little did I know that because my father wasn't governor of Maine and I didn't go to Dartmouth College, my chance wasn't going to be the same as the next guy's, that three weeks later I'd be as good as dead. Because I didn't commune with nature, you see, up there in the Maine woods. Because while Hewlett was sitting on his ass studying to lie at Dartmouth College, I was serving this country in *two* wars. Two years in World War II and then I get called back for Korea! But this is all in my book. Whether it's all going to get in the musical, well, how could it? Face facts. You know this country better than anybody. There are people that, as soon as word gets out that I'm working on what I'm working on with Marty Paté, who are going to put the pressure on him to drop me like a hot potato. I wouldn't even rule out payoffs from the networks. I wouldn't rule out the F.C.C. taking him aside. I can see Nixon himself getting involved to quash it. I'm supposed to be a disturbed and unstable person, you see. That's what they'll tell Marty to scare him off. That's what they told everybody, including me, including the parents of my stupid fiancée, including finally a special subcommittee from the United States House of Representatives. That was the story when I refused to go along with being dethroned for no reason after only three weeks. Bateman was practically in tears from worrying about my mental stability. 'If you knew the discussions we have had about your character, Alvin. If you knew the surprise it has been to us, that you have not turned out to be the trustworthy fellow we all so believed in. We're so worried about you,' he tells me, 'we've decided to pay for a psychiatrist for you. We want you to see Dr. Eisenberg until you have gotten over your neurosis and are yourself again.' 'Absolutely,' Schachtman says,

'I see Dr. Eisenberg, why shouldn't Alvin see
Dr. Eisenberg? This organization is not going
to save a few lousy dollars at the expense of
Alvin's mental stability.' This is how they
were going to discredit me, by setting me up
as a nut. Well, that tune changed fast. Because, one, I wasn't going in for any psychi-
atric treatment, and two, what I wanted was
a written agreement from them, guarantee-
ing that first Hewlett and I fight to a draw
for three consecutive weeks and *then* I leave.
And one month later, by popular request, a
rematch, which he would win by a hair in the
last second. But not on the subject of Americana. I was not going to let a goy beat a Jew
again on that, not while the entire country
was watching. Let him beat me on a subject
like Trees, I said, which is their specialty and
doesn't mean anything to anybody anyway.
But I refuse to let the Jewish people go down
on prime-time TV as not knowing their
Americana. Either I had all that in writing,
I said, or I would go to the press with the
truth, including the stuff about the little girl
with the braids and how they set her up too,
first with the answers and then to take a dive.
You should have heard Bateman then, and
how much he was worried about my mental

condition. 'Do you want to destroy my career, Alvin? Why? Why me? Why Schachtman and Bateman, after all we've done for you? Didn't we get your teeth cleaned? Sharp new suits? A dermatologist? Is this the way you plan to pay us back, by going up to people in the street and telling them Hewlett is a fake? Alvin, all these threats, all this blackmail. Alvin, we are not hardened criminals—we are in show business. You cannot ask random questions of people and have a show. We want 'Smart Money' to be something the people of America can look forward to every week with excitement. But if you just ask random questions, you know you would have nobody knowing the answer two times in a row. You would have just failure, and failure does not make entertainment. You have to have a plot, like in *Hamlet* or anything else first-class. To the audience, Alvin, maybe you are only contestants. But to us you are far more. You are performers. You are artists. Artists making art for America, just the way Shakespeare made it in his day for England. And that is with a plot, and conflict, and suspense, and a resolution. And the resolution is that you should lose to Hewlett, and we have a new face on the show. Does Hamlet get up from the stage and say I don't want to die at the end of the play? No, his part is over and he lies there. That is the difference, in point of fact, between schlock and art. Schlock goes every which way and couldn't care less about anything but the buck, and art is *controlled,* art is *managed,* art is *always* rigged. That is how it takes hold of the human heart.' And this is where Schachtman pipes up and tells me that they are going to make a sportscaster out of me, as a reward, if I keep my mouth shut and go down for the count. So I did. But did they, *did they,* after telling me that *I* wasn't the one to be trusted?"

"No," said Zuckerman.

"You can say that again. Three weeks, and that was it. They cleaned my teeth and they kissed my ass, and for three weeks I was their hero. The mayor had me into his office. Did I tell you that? 'You have placed the name of the city of Newark before the whole country.' He said this to me in front of the City Council, who clapped. I went to Lindy's and signed a picture of myself for their wall. Milton Berle came up to my table and asked me some questions, as a gag. One week they're taking me for cheesecake to Lindy's and the next week they tell me I'm washed up. And call me names, into the bargain. 'Alvin,' Schachtman says to me, 'is this what you're going to turn out to be, you who has done so much good for Newark and your family and the Marines and the Jews? Just another exhibitionist who has no motive but greed?' I was furious. 'What is your motive, Schachtman? What is Bateman's motive? What is the sponsor's motive? What is the network's motive?' And the truth is that greed had nothing to do with it. It was by this time my self-respect. As a man! As a war veteran! As a war veteran twice over! As a Newarker! As a Jew! What they were saying, you understand, was that all these things that made up Alvin Pepler and his pride in himself were unadulterated crap next to a Hewlett Lincoln. One hundred and seventy-three thousand dollars, that's what he wound up with, that fake. Thirty thousand fan letters. Interviewed by more than five hundred newsmen from around the world. Another face? Another *religion,* that's the ugly truth of it! This hurt me, Nathan. I am hurt still, and it isn't just egotistically either, I swear to you. This is why I'm fighting them, why I'll fight them right to the end, until my true story is before the American public. If Paté is my chance, then don't you see, I *have* to jump for it. If it has to be a musical first and *then* the book, then that's the way it has to be until my name is cleared!"

Perspiration streamed from beneath his dark rain hat, and with the handkerchief Zuckerman had given him earlier, he reached up to wipe it off—enabling Zuckerman to step away from the street-corner mailbox where Pepler had him pinned. In fifteen minutes, the two Newarkers had traveled one block.

Across the street from where they stood was a Baskin-Robbins ice-cream parlor. The evening was cool, yet customers walked in and out as though it were already summertime. Inside the lighted store there was a small crowd waiting at the counter to be served.

Because he didn't know how to begin to reply, and probably because Pepler was perspiring so, Zuckerman heard himself ask, "What about an ice cream?" Of course, what Pepler would have preferred from Zuckerman was this: *You were robbed, ruined, brutally betrayed*—Carnovsky's *author commits his strength to the redress of Pepler's grievance.* But the best Zuckerman could do was to offer an ice-cream snack. He doubted if anyone could do better.

"Oh, forgive me," said Pepler. "I'm sorry for this. Of course you've got to be starving, with me talking your ear off and then eating half your dinner in the bargain. Forgive me, please, if I got carried away on this subject. Meeting you has just thrown me for a loop. I don't usually go off half-cocked like this, telling everybody my troubles out on the street. I'm so quiet with people, their first impression is I'm death warmed over. Someone like Miss Gibraltar," he said, reddening, "thinks I'm practically a deaf-mute. Hey, let *me* buy *you*."

"No, no, not necessary."

But as they crossed the street, Pepler insisted. "After the pleasure you've given to me as a reader? After the earful I just gave you?" Refusing even to let Zuckerman enter the store with his money, Pepler cried, "Yes, yes, my treat, absolutely. For our great Newark writer who has cast his spell over the entire country! For that great magician who has pulled a living, breathing Carnovsky out of his artistic hat! Who has hypnotized the U.S.A.! Here's to the author of that wonderful best-selling book!" And then, suddenly, he was looking at Zuckerman as tenderly as a father on an outing with his darling baby boy. "Do you want jimmies on top, Nathan?"

"Sure."

"And flavor?"

"Chocolate is fine."

"Both dips?"

"Fine."

Comically tapping at his skull to indicate that the order was tucked safely away in the photographic memory that was once the pride of Newark, the nation, and the Jews, Pepler hurried into the store. Zuckerman waited out on the pavement alone.

But for what?

Would Mary Mapes Dodge wait like this for an ice-cream cone?

Would Frank Sinatra?

Would a ten-year-old child with any brains?

As though passing the time on a pleasant evening, he practiced ambling toward the corner. Then he ran. Down the side street, unpursued.

2

"You're Nathan Zuckerman"

Though his new number was unlisted, Zuckerman paid a service thirty dollars a month to answer for him and find out who was calling. "How's our gorgeous writer?" asked Rochelle, when later that evening he phoned for the day's messages. She was the manager of the service and treated customers she'd never laid eyes on like old friends. "When are you going to drop around and give the girls a thrill?" Zuckerman replied that he gave them enough thrills when they listened in on his line. Good-natured banter, yet he also believed it was true. But better their eavesdropping than him having to fend off the unlikely people who seemed to have no trouble getting his unlisted number. There was supposed to be an outfit supplying the unlisted numbers of celebrities for twenty-five bucks a great name. Could even be in cahoots with his answering service. Could even be his answering service.

"The Rollmops King called. He's gone on you, hon. You're the Jewish Charles Dickens. Those were his words. You've hurt his feelings, Mr. Zuckerman, by not calling back." The Rollmops King thought Zuckerman should endorse appetizer snacks on a television commercial—an actress could play Mrs. Zuckerman if his own mother was unavailable for the job. "I can't help him out. Next message." "But you like herring—it's in the book." "Everybody likes herring, Rochelle." "Why not do it then?" "Next message." "The Italian. Twice in the morning, twice in the afternoon." If Zuckerman did not grant him an interview, the Italian, a Rome journalist, was going to be out of a job. "Do you think that's true, doll?" "I hope so." "He says he doesn't understand why you should treat him like this. He got very emotional when I told him I was only the service. You know what I'm afraid of? That he is going to make it up, a personal interview with Nathan Zuckerman, and they'll pass it off in Rome as the real thing." "Is that something he suggested as a possibility?" "He suggested a lot of possibilities. You know when an Italian gets going." "Anyone else ring?" "He left a question, Mr. Zuckerman. One question." "I've answered my last question. Who else?"

Laura's was the name he was waiting for.

"Melanie. Three times." "No last name?" "No. Just tell him Melanie collect from Rhode Island. He'll know." "It's a big state—I don't." "You would if you accepted the charges. You'd know everything then," said Rochelle, turning throaty, "for only a dollar. After, you could deduct it." "I'd rather bank it." She liked that. "I don't blame you. You know how to accumulate it, Mr. Zuckerman. I'll bet the I.R.S. doesn't take it from you like they do from me." "They take what they can get." "But what about tax shelters? Are you by any chance on to macadamia nuts?" "No." "How about cattle?" "Rochelle, I can't help the Rollmops King or the Italian or Melanie, and much as I'd like to, I can't help you. I don't know anything about these shelters." "No shelters? In your bracket? You must be paying seventy cents back on your top dollar. What do you do, take 'em to the cleaners on entertainment?" "My entertaining is a grave

61

disappointment to my accountant." "What *do* you do then? No shelters, no entertainment, and on top of your ordinary tax, Johnson's surcharge. Pardon my saying it, but if this is really so, Mr. Zuckerman, Uncle Sam should get down on his knees and kiss your ass."

More or less what the investment specialist had told him earlier that day. He was a trim, tall, cultivated gentleman not much older than Zuckerman, who had a painting by Picasso hanging on his office wall. Mary Schevitz, sparring partner and wife to Zuckerman's agent, André, and would-be mother to André's clientele, had been hoping that Bill Wallace would influence Nathan by talking to him about money in his Brahmin accent. Wallace too had written a best-selling book, a witty attack on the securities establishment by a card-carrying Racquet Club member. According to Mary, a copy of Wallace's exposé, *Profits Without Honor,* could do wonders for the conscience pangs of all those well-heeled Jewish investors who liked to consider themselves skeptical of the system.

You couldn't put anything over on Mary; not even on upper Park Avenue was she out of touch with the lower depths. Her mother had been an Irish washerwoman in the

Bronx—*the* Irish washerwoman, to hear her tell it—and she had Zuckerman pegged as someone whose secret desire was to make it big with the genteel WASPs. That Laura's family were genteel WASPs, by washerwoman standards, was only the beginning. "You think," Mary told him, "that if you pretend not to care about money, nobody will mistake you for a Newark Yid." "I'm afraid there are other distinguishing features." "Don't cloud the issue with Jewish jokes. You know what I mean. A kike."

The Brahmin investment counselor couldn't have been more charming, Zuckerman couldn't have been more Brahmin, and the Blue Period Picasso couldn't have cared less: Hear no money, see no money, think no money. The painting's theme of tragic suffering absolutely purified the air. Mary had a point. You couldn't imagine they were talking about what people begged for, lied for, murdered for, or even just worked for, nine to five. It was as though they were talking about nothing.

"André says you're more conservative in financial affairs than in your fiction."

Though Zuckerman was not so well-dressed as the investment counselor, he was, for the occasion, no less soft-spoken. "In the books I've got nothing to lose."

"No, no. You're just a sensible man, behaving as any sensible man would. You know nothing about money, you know you know nothing about money, and understandably you're reluctant to act."

For the next hour, as though it were opening day at the Harvard Business School, Wallace told Zuckerman about the fundamentals of capital investment and what happens to money when it is left too long in a shoe.

When Zuckerman got up to go, Wallace said mildly, "If you should ever want any help..." An afterthought.

"I will indeed..."

They shook hands, to signify that they understood not only each other but how to bend the world their way. It wasn't like this in Zuckerman's study.

"It may not seem so to look at me, but I'm familiar by now with the sort of goals artists set for themselves. I've tried to help out several of you people over the years."

Self-effacement. You people were three of the biggest names in American painting.

Wallace smiled. "None of them knew anything about stocks and bonds, but today they're all financially secure. So will their heirs be tomorrow. And not just from selling pictures. They no more want to worry about peddling than you do. Why should you? You should get on with your work, totally indifferent to the marketplace, and for as long as the work requires. 'When I think that I have gathered my fruit I shall not refuse to sell it, nor shall I forfeit hand-clapping if it is good. In the meantime I do not wish to fleece the public. That's all there is to it.' Flaubert."

Not bad. Especially if the Schevitzes hadn't tipped Wallace off beforehand to the millionaire's soft spot.

"If we begin swapping great quotations disavowing everything but the integrity of my singularly pure vocation," said Zuckerman, "we'll be here till midnight tomorrow. Let me go home and talk it over with the shoe."

Of course the one he wanted to talk it over with was Laura. There was everything to talk over with Laura, but her good sense he had lost, just when his was being challenged as never before. If he had consulted first with levelheaded Laura about leaving her, he might never have left. If they had sat down in his study, each with a yellow pad and a pencil, they could have laid out together in their usual orderly and practical way the utterly predictable consequences of starting life anew on the eve of the publication of *Carnovsky*. But he had left for the new life because, among other things, he could not bear to sit down anymore with a pad and a pencil to lay things out with her in their usual way.

It was more than two months since the movers had carried away from the downtown Bank Street floor-through his typewriter, his worktable, his orthopedic typing chair, and four file cabinets crammed with abandoned manuscripts, forgotten journals, reading notes, news clippings, and with hefty folders of correspondence dating back to college. They also carried away, by their estimate, nearly half a ton of books. While fair-minded Laura insisted that Nathan take with him half of everything they had accumulated together—down to towels, silverware, and blankets—he insisted on taking nothing but the furnishings from his study. They were both in tears and holding hands while the issue was debated.

Carrying his books from one life into the next was nothing new to Zuckerman. He had left his family for Chicago in 1949 carrying in his suitcase the annotated works of Thomas

Wolfe and *Roget's Thesaurus*. Four years later, age twenty, he left Chicago with five cartons of the classics, bought secondhand out of his spending money, to be stored in his parents' attic while he served two years in the Army. In 1960, when he was divorced from Betsy, there were thirty cartons to be packed from shelves no longer his; in 1965, when he was divorced from Virginia, there were just under sixty to cart away; in 1969, he left Bank Street with eighty-one boxes of books. To house them, new shelves twelve feet high had been built to his specifications along three walls of his new study; but though two months had passed, and though books were generally the first possession to find their proper place in his home, they remained this time in their boxes. Half a million pages untouched, unturned. The only book that seemed to exist was his own. And whenever he tried to forget it, someone reminded him.

Zuckerman had contracted for the carpentry, bought a color TV and an Oriental rug, all on the day he moved uptown. He was determined, despite the farewell tears, to be determined. But the Oriental rug constituted his first and his last stab at "decor." Purchases since had fallen way off: a pot, a pan, a dish, a towel for the dish, a shower curtain, a canvas chair, a Parsons table, a garbage pail—one thing at a time, and only when it became a necessity. After weeks on the fold-up cot from his old study, after weeks of wondering if leaving Laura hadn't been a terrible mistake, he gathered his strength and bought a real bed. At Bloomingdale's, while he stretched out on his back to see which brand was the firmest—while word traveled round the floor that Carnovsky, in person, could be seen trying out mattresses for God only knew who else or how many—Zuckerman told himself, Never mind, nothing lost, this hasn't changed a thing: if the day ever comes for the movers to truck the books back downtown, they'll take the new double bed too. Laura and he could use it to replace the one on which they had been sleeping together, or not sleeping together, for nearly three years.

Oh, how Laura was loved and admired! Heartbroken mothers, thwarted fathers, desperate girlfriends, all regularly sent her presents out of gratitude for the support she was giving their dear ones hiding in Canada from the draft. The homemade preserves, she and Zuckerman ate at breakfast; the boxes of chocolate, she circulated among the neighborhood children; the touching items of knitted apparel, she took to the Quakers who ran the Peace and Reconciliation Thrift Shop on MacDougal Street. And the cards sent with the presents, the moving, anguished notes and letters, she kept as cherished memorabilia in her files. For safety's sake, against the possibility of an F.B.I. break-in, the files were stored with Rosemary Ditson, the elderly retired schoolteacher who lived alone in the basement apartment next door and who also loved her. Rosemary's health and general welfare Laura took as her responsibility only days after she and Zuckerman moved onto the block, when Laura observed the frail, disheveled woman trying to descend the steep cement stairwell without dropping her groceries or breaking a hip.

How could you *not* love generous, devoted, thoughtful, kindhearted Laura? How could *he* not? Yet during their last months together in the Bank Street floor-through, virtually all they had left in common was the rented Xerox machine at the foot of their tub in the big tiled bathroom.

Laura's law office was in the parlor at the front of the apartment, his study in the spare room on the quiet courtyard at the back. During an ordinary productive day he sometimes had to wait his turn at the bathroom door while Laura rushed to photocopy pages going out in the next mail. If Zuckerman had to copy something especially long, he would try to hold off until she took her late-night bath, so they could chat together while the pages dropped. One afternoon they even had intercourse on the bath mat beside the Xerox machine, but that was back when it was first installed. To be running into each other during the course of the day, manuscript pages in hand, was still something of a novelty then; many things were a novelty then. But by their last year they hardly even had intercourse in bed. Laura's face was as sweet as ever, her breasts were as full as ever, and who could question that her heart was in the right place? Who could question her virtue, her rectitude, her purpose? But by the third year he had come to wonder whether Laura's purpose wasn't the shield behind which he was still hiding his own, even from himself.

Though looking after her war resisters, deserters, and conscientious objectors kept her working days, nights, and weekends, she managed nonetheless to note in her calendar book the birthday of every child living on

Bank Street, and would slip a little present into the family mailbox on the morning of the event: "From Laura and Nathan Z." The same for their friends, whose anniversaries and birthdays she also recorded there along with the dates she was to fly to Toronto or appear at the courthouse in Foley Square. Any child that she encountered in the supermarket or on the bus was invariably taken aside and taught by Laura how to make an origami flying horse. Once Zuckerman watched her negotiate the length of a crowded subway car to point out to a straphanger that his billfold was protruding from his back pocket—protruding, Zuckerman observed, because he was a drunk in rags and most likely had found it in somebody's leavings or lifted it off another drunk. Though Laura wore not a trace of makeup, though her only adornment was a tiny enamel dove pinned to her trench coat, the drunk seemed to take her for a sassy prostitute on the prowl, and clutching at his trousers, he told her to piss off. Zuckerman said afterward that maybe he'd had a point. Surely she could leave the drunks to the Salvation Army. They argued about her do-goodism. Zuckerman suggested there might be limits. "Why?" asked Laura flatly. This was in January, just three months before the publication of *Carnovsky*.

The following week, with nothing to keep him locked behind the study door where usually he spent his days complicating life for himself on paper, he packed a suitcase and began again to complicate his life in the world. With his page proofs and his suitcase, he moved into a hotel. His feeling for Laura was dead. Writing this book had finished it off. Or maybe finishing the book had given him time to look up at last and see what had died; that was the way it usually worked with his wives. The woman's too good for you, he told himself, reading page proofs on the bed in his hotel room. She is the reputable face that you turn toward the reputable, the face you have been turning toward them all your life. It isn't even Laura's virtue that bores you to tears—it's the reputable, responsible, drearily virtuous face that's your own. It should bore you. It is a goddamn disgrace. Coldhearted betrayer of the most intimate confessions, cutthroat caricaturist of your own loving parents, graphic reporter of encounters with women to whom you have been deeply bound by trust, by sex, by love—no, the virtue racket ill becomes you. It is simply weakness—childish, shame-ridden, indefensible weakness—that condemns you to prove about yourself a point that you only subvert by everything that enlivens your writing, *so stop trying to prove it*. Hers is the cause of righteousness, yours the art of depiction. It really shouldn't take half a lifetime for someone with your brains to figure out the difference.

In March he moved into the new apartment in the East Eighties, thereby separating himself by much of Manhattan from Laura's missionary zeal and moral reputation.

After finishing with the answering service, and before starting on his mail, Zuckerman got out the telephone book to look up "Paté, Martin." There was no such listing. Couldn't find a "Paté Productions" either, not in the regular directory or in the Yellow Pages.

He dialed the answering service again.

"Rochelle, I'm trying to locate the actress Gayle Gibraltar."

"Lucky girl."

"Do you have some kind of show-business directory there?"

"Got all a man could want here, Mr. Zuckerman. I'll take a look." When she came back on the line, she said, "No Gayle Gibraltar, Mr. Zuckerman. Closest I've got is a Roberta Plymouth. You sure that's her professional and not her real name?"

"It doesn't sound real to me. But not much does lately. She was just in some Sardinian film."

"One minute, Mr. Zuckerman." But when she came back on, there was still nothing to report. "I can't find her anywhere. How did you meet her? Party?"

"I haven't met her. She's the friend of a friend."

"I get it."

"He tells me she was once Playmate of the Month."

"Okay, let's try that." But she couldn't find a Gibraltar in any of the model listings either. "Describe her to me, Mr. Zuckerman, physically."

"No need," he said, and hung up.

He opened the directory to "Perlmutter." No "Martin" listed. And of sixteen other assorted Perlmutters, none residing on East Sixty-second Street.

The mail. On to the mail. You are getting stirred up over nothing. Undoubtedly listed as "Sardinian Enterprises." Not that there is any reason to go see. No more reason than to run away. Stop running away. From what in God's name are you in flight? Stop taking every attention as an intrusion on your privacy, as an insult to your dignity—even worse, as a threat to life and limb. You are not even that big a celebrity. Let's not forget that most of the country, most of the *city*, wouldn't care if you walked around with your name and your unlisted number on a sandwich board. Even among writers, even among writers of some pretensions to seriousness, you are still no titan. I am not saying that you should be any less confounded by a change like this, I am only saying that being known, even being known for the moment as mildly notorious—mildly, for sure, by comparison with Charles Manson, or even with Mick Jagger or Jean Genet—

The mail.

He had decided that it would be better to end rather than to begin the day with his mail if he was ever going to get back to work; best to ignore the mail completely if he was ever going to get back to work. But how much more could he ignore, dismiss, or try to elude, before he became one with the stiffs at the undertaker's down the street?

The phone! Laura! He had left three messages in three days and heard nothing. But he was sure it was Laura, it had to be Laura, she was no less lonely or lost than he was. Yet, to be on the safe side, he waited for the service to pick up before quietly lifting the receiver.

Rochelle had to ask the caller several times to make himself more intelligible. Zuckerman, silently listening, couldn't understand him either. The Italian in pursuit of his interview? The Rollmops King hungry for his commercial? A man trying to speak like an animal, or an animal trying to speak like a man? Hard to tell.

"Again, *please*," said Rochelle.

In touch with Zuckerman. Urgent. Put him on.

Rochelle asked him to leave a name and number.

Put him on.

Again she asked for a name and the connection was broken.

Zuckerman spoke up. "Hello, I'm on the line. What was that all about?"

"Oh, hello, Mr. Zuckerman."

"What *was* that? Do you have any idea?"

"It could just be a pervert, Mr. Zuckerman. I wouldn't worry."

She worked nights, she should know. "Don't you think it was somebody trying to disguise his voice?"

"Could be. Or on drugs. I wouldn't worry, Mr. Zuckerman."

The mail.

Eleven letters tonight—one from André's West Coast office and ten (still pretty much the daily average) forwarded to him in a large envelope from his publisher. Of these, six were addressed to Nathan Zuckerman, three to Gilbert Carnovsky; one, sent in care of the publishing house, was addressed simply to "The Enemy of the Jews" and had been forwarded to him unopened. They were awfully smart down in that mailroom.

The only letters at all tempting were those marked "Photo Do Not Bend," and there was none in this batch. He had received five so far, the most intriguing still the first, from a young New Jersey secretary who had enclosed a color snapshot of herself, reclining in black underwear on her back lawn in Livingston, reading a novel by John Updike. An overturned tricycle in the corner of the picture seemed to belie the single status she claimed for herself in the attached curriculum vitae. However, investigation with his Compact Oxford English Dictionary magnifying glass revealed no sign on the body that it had borne a child, or the least little care in the world. Could it be that the owner of the tricycle had just happened to be pedaling by and dismounted in haste when summoned to snap the picture? Zuckerman studied the photograph on and off for the better part of a morning, before forwarding it to Massachusetts, along with a note asking if Updike would be good enough to reroute photographs of Zuckerman readers mistakenly sent to him.

From André's office a column clipped out of *Variety*, initialed by the West Coast secretary, whose admiration for his work led her to send Zuckerman items from the show-business press that he might otherwise miss. The latest was underlined in red. "...Independent Bob 'Sleepy' Lagoon paid close to a million for Nathan Zuckerman's unfinished sequel to the smasheroo..."

Oh, did he? What sequel? Who is Lagoon? Friend of Paté and Gibraltar? Why does she send me this stuff!

"—unfinished sequel—"

Oh, throw it away, laugh it off, you keep ducking when you should be smiling.

Dear Gilbert Carnovsky:

Forget about satisfaction. The question is not is Carnovsky happy, or even, does Carnovsky have the right to happiness? The question to ask yourself is this: Have I achieved all that could be done by me? A man must live independent of the barometer of happiness, or fail. A man must...

Dear Mr. Zuckerman:

Il faut laver son linge sale en famille!

Dear Mr. Zuckerman:

This letter is written in memory of those who suffered the horror of the Concentration Camps...

Dear Mr. Zuckerman:

It is hardly possible to write of Jews with more bile and contempt and hatred...

The phone.

He reached for it this time without thinking—the way he used to get on the bus and go out for his dinner and walk by himself through the park. "Lorelei!" he cried into the receiver. As if that would summon her forth, and all their wonderful Bank Street boredom. His life back under control. His reputable face toward the world.

"Don't hang up, Zuckerman. Don't hang up unless you're looking for bad trouble."

The character he'd overheard with Rochelle. The hoarse, high-pitched voice, with the vaguely imbecilic intonation. Sounded like some large barking animal, yes, like some up-and-coming seal who had broken into human speech. It was the speech, supposedly, of the thickheaded.

"I have an important message for you, Zuckerman. You better listen carefully."

"Who is this?"

"I want some of the money."

"Which money?"

"Come off it. You're Nathan Zuckerman, Zuckerman. Your money."

"Look, this isn't entertaining, whoever you are. You can get in trouble like this, you know, even if the imitation is meant to be humorous. What is it you're supposed to be, some punch-drunk palooka or Marlon Brando?" It was all getting much too ridiculous. Hang up. Say nothing more and hang up.

But he couldn't—not after he heard the voice saying, "Your mother lives at 1167 Silver Crescent Drive in Miami Beach. She lives in a condominium across the hall from your old cousin Essie and her husband, Mr. Metz, the bridge player. They live in 402, your mother lives in 401. A cleaning woman named Olivia comes in on Tuesdays. Friday nights your mother has dinner with Essie and her crowd at the Century Beach. Sunday mornings she goes to the Temple to help with the bazaar. Thursday afternoons there is her club. They sit by the pool and play canasta: Bea Wirth, Sylvia Adlerstein, Lily Sobol, Lily's sister-in-law Flora, and your mother. Otherwise she is visiting your old man in the nursing home. If you don't want her to disappear, you'll listen to what I have to say, and you won't waste time with cracks about my voice. This happens to be the voice that I was born with. Not everybody is perfect like you."

"Who is this?"

"I'm a fan. I admit it, despite the insults. I'm an admirer, Zuckerman. I'm somebody who has been following your career for years

81

now. I've been waiting for a long time for you to hit it big with the public. I knew it would happen one day. It had to. You have a real talent. You make things come alive for people. Though frankly I don't think this is your best book."

"Oh, don't you?"

"Go ahead, put me down, but the depth isn't there. Flash, yes; depth, no. This is something you had to write to make a new beginning. So it's incomplete, it's raw, it's pyrotechnics. But I understand that. I even admire it. To try things a new way is the only way to grow. I see you growing enormously as a writer, if you don't lose your guts."

"And you'll grow with me, is that the idea?"

The mirthless laugh of the stage villain. "Haw. Haw. Haw."

Zuckerman hung up. Should have as soon as he heard who it was and was not. More of what he simply must become inured to. Trivial, meaningless, only to be expected—he hadn't, after all, written *Tom Swift*. Yes, Rochelle had the right idea. "Only some pervert, Mr. Zuckerman. I wouldn't worry."

Yet he wondered if he shouldn't dial the police. What *was* worrying was all that his caller had said about his mother in Florida.

But since the *Life* cover story, and the attention she subsequently got from the Miami papers, details on Nathan Zuckerman's mother were not so hard to come by, really, if you happened to be looking. She had herself successfully resisted all the determined efforts to flatter, beguile, and bully her into an "exclusive" interview; it was lonely Flora Sobol, Lily's recently widowed sister-in-law, who'd been unable to hold out against the onslaught. Though afterward Flora insisted she had spoken with the newspaperwoman for only a few minutes on the phone, a half-page article had nonetheless appeared in the weekend amusement section of the *Miami Herald,* under the title, "I Play Canasta with Carnovsky's Mother." Accompanying the article, a picture of lonely, pretty, aging Flora and her two Pekinese.

Some six weeks before publication—when he could begin to see the size of the success that was coming, and had intimations that the Hallelujah Chorus might not be entirely a pleasure from beginning to end—Zuckerman had flown down to Miami to prepare his mother for the reporters. As a result of what he told her over dinner, she was unable to get to sleep that night and had to cross the hall to Essie's apartment finally and ask if she could come in for a tranquilizer and a serious talk.

I am very proud of my son and that's all I have to say. Thank you so much and goodbye.

This was the line that she might be wisest to take when the journalists began phoning her. Of course, if she didn't mind the personal publicity, if she *wanted* her name in the papers—

"Darling, it's me you're talking to, not Elizabeth Taylor."

Whereupon, over their seafood dinner, he pretended that he was a newspaper reporter who had nothing better to do than call her up to ask about Nathan's toilet training. She in turn had to pretend that some such thing was going to be happening every day once his new novel appeared in the bookstores.

"'But what about being Carnovsky's mother? Let's face it, Mrs. Zuckerman, this is who you are now.'"

"'I have two fine sons I'm very proud of.'"

"That's good, Ma. If you want to put it that way, that's all right. Though you don't even have to say that much if you don't want to. You can just laugh, if you like."

"In his face?"

"No, no—no need to insult anyone. That wouldn't be a good idea either. I mean, just lightly laugh it off. Or say nothing at all. Silence is fine, and most effective."

"All right."

"'Mrs. Zuckerman?'"

"'Yes?'"

"'The whole world wants to know. They've read in your boy's book all about Gilbert Carnovsky and his mother, and now they want to know from you, how does it feel to be so famous?'"

"'I couldn't tell you. Thank you for your interest in my son.'"

"Ma, good enough. But the point I'm making is that you can say goodbye any time. They never quit, these people, so all you have to do is say goodbye and hang up."

"'Goodbye.'"

"'But wait a minute, not yet, please, Mrs. Zuckerman! I've got to come back with this assignment. I've got a new baby, a new house, I have bills to pay—a story about Nathan could mean a big raise.'"

"'Oh, I'm sure you'll get one anyway.'"

"Mother, that is excellent. Keep going."

"'Thank you for calling. Goodbye.'"

"'Mrs. Zuckerman, just two minutes off the record?'"

"'Thank you, goodbye.'"

"'*One* minute. One *line*. Won't you please, Mrs. Z., one little line for my article about your remarkable son?'"

"'Goodbye, goodbye now.'"

"Ma, the truth is, you don't even have to keep saying goodbye. That's hard for a courteous person to understand. But by this time you could go ahead and hang up without feeling that you've slighted anyone."

Over dessert he put her through it again, just to be sure she was ready. Any wonder that by midnight she needed a Valium?

He knew nothing about how disturbing a visit it had been until his last trip to Miami just three weeks ago. First they went to visit his father in the nursing home. Dr. Zuckerman could not really speak comprehensibly since the last stroke—just half-formed words and truncated syllables—and there were times when he didn't know at first who she was. He looked at her and moved his mouth to say "Molly," the name of his dead sister. That you could no longer tell just how much of anything he knew was what made her daily visits such hell. Nonetheless, she seemed that day to be looking better than she had in years, if not quite the curly-headed young madonna cuddling her somber first-born son in the 1935 seaside photograph framed on his father's bed table, certainly not so done-in as to frighten you about *her* health. Ever since the trial of caring for his father had begun for her four years back—four years during which he wouldn't let her out of his sight—she had been looking far less like the energetic and indomitable mother from whom Nathan had inherited the lively burnish of his eyes (and the mild comedy of his profile) than like his gaunt, silent, defeated grandmother, the spectral widow of the tyrannical shopkeeper, her father.

When they got home, she had to lie down on the sofa with a cold cloth on her forehead.

"You look better, though, Ma."

"It's easier with him there. I hate to say it, Nathan. But I'm just beginning to feel a little like myself." He had been in the nursing home now for some twelve weeks.

"Of course it's easier," said her son. "That was the idea."

"Today was not a good day for him. I'm sorry you saw him like this."

"That's all right."

"But he knew who you were, I'm sure."

Zuckerman wasn't so sure, but said, "I know he did."

"I only wish he knew how wonderful you're doing. All this success. But it's really too much, dear, to explain in his condition."

"And it's all right too if he doesn't know. The best thing is to let him rest comfortably."

Here she lowered the cloth over her eyes. She was beginning to weep, and didn't want him to see.

"What is it, Ma?"

"It's that I'm so relieved, really, about you. I never told you, I kept it to myself, but the day you flew down to tell me all that was going to happen because of the book, I thought—well, I thought you were headed for a terrible fall. I thought maybe it was because you didn't have Daddy now as somebody who was always there behind you—that you didn't on your own know which way to turn. And then Mr. Metz"—the new husband of Dr. Zuckerman's old cousin Essie—"he said it sounded to him like 'delusions of grandeur.' He doesn't mean any harm, Mr. Metz—he goes every week to read Daddy 'The News in Review' from the Sunday paper. He's a wonderful man, but that was his opinion. And then Essie started in. She said that all his life your daddy has had delusions of grandeur—that even when they were children together he wasn't happy unless he was telling everybody how to live and butting in on what was none of his business. This is Essie, mind you, with that mouth she has on her. I said to her, 'Essie, let's leave your argument with Victor out of this. Since the man can't even talk anymore to make himself understood, maybe that should put a stop to it.' But what they said scared the daylights out of me, sweetheart. I thought, Maybe it's true—something in his makeup that he got from his father. But I should have known better. My big boy is nobody's fool. The way you are taking all this is just wonderful. People down here ask me, 'What is he like now with his picture in all the papers?' And I tell them that you are somebody who never put on airs and never will."

"But, Ma, you mustn't let them get you down with this business about Carnovsky's mother."

All at once she was like a child at whose

bedside he was sitting, a child who'd been cruelly teased at school and had come home in tears, running a fever.

Smiling bravely, removing the cloth and showing him the burnish of his eyes in her head, she said, "I try not to."

"But it's hard."

"But sometimes it's hard, darling, I have to admit it. The newspapers I can deal with, thanks to you. You would be proud of me."

To the end of her sentence he silently affixed the word "Papa." He had known her papa, and how he'd made her and her sisters toe the line. First the domineering father, then the domineering, father-dominated husband. For parents Zuckerman could claim the world's most obedient daughter and son.

"Oh, you should hear me, Nathan. I'm courteous, of course, but I cut them dead, exactly the way you said. But with people I meet socially it's different. People say to me—and right out, without a second thought—'I didn't know you were crazy like that, Selma.' I tell them I'm not. I tell them what you told me: that it's a story, that she is a character in a book. So they say, 'Why does he write a story like that, unless it's true?' And then really what can I say—that they'll believe?"

"Silence, Ma. Don't say anything."

"But you can't, Nathan. If you say nothing, it doesn't work. Then they're sure they're right."

"Then tell them your boy is a madman. Tell them you're not responsible for the things that come into his head. Tell them you're lucky he doesn't make up things even worse. That's not far from the truth. Mother, you know you are yourself and not Mrs. Carnovsky, and I know you are yourself and not Mrs. Carnovsky. You and I know that it was very nearly heaven thirty years ago."

"Oh, darling, is that true?"

"Absolutely."

"But that isn't what the book says. I mean, that isn't what people think, who read it. They think it even if they *don't* read it."

"There's nothing to do about what people think, except to pay as little attention as possible."

"At the pool, when I'm not there, they say you won't have anything to do with me. Can you believe that? They tell this to Essie. Some of them say you won't have anything to do with me, some of them say I won't have anything to do with you, and the others say I'm living on Easy Street because of all the money you send me. I'm supposed to have a Cadillac, courtesy of my millionaire son. What do you think of that? Essie tells them that I don't even drive, but that doesn't stop them. The Cadillac has a colored driver."

"Next they'll be saying he's your lover."

"I wouldn't be surprised if they say it already. They say everything. Every day I hear another story. Some I wouldn't even repeat. Thank God your father isn't able to hear them."

"Maybe Essie shouldn't pass on to you what people say. If you want, I'll tell her that."

"There was a discussion of your book at our Jewish Center."

"Was there?"

"Darling, Essie says it is already the main topic of discussion at every Jewish wedding, bar mitzvah, social club, women's club, sisterhood meeting, and closing luncheon in America. I don't know the details about everywhere else, but at our Center it wound up a discussion of you. Essie and Mr. Metz went. I thought I was better off minding my own business at home. Somebody named Posner gave the lecture. Then there was the discussion. Do you know him, Nathan? Essie says he's a boy your age."

"I don't know him, no."

"Afterward Essie went up and gave him a piece of her mind. You know Essie, when she gets going. She's driven Daddy crazy all his life, but she is your biggest defender. Of course she's never read a book in her life, but that wouldn't stop Essie. She says you are just like her, and you were even when you wrote about her and Meema Chaya's will. You say what's on your mind and the hell with everybody else."

"That's Essie and me, Mama."

She smiled. "Always a joke." Whether the joke had eased her of her burden was something else. "Nathan, Mr. Metz's daughter was down here last week to see him, and she did the sweetest thing. She's a schoolteacher in Philadelphia, pretty as a picture, and she took me aside in the sweetest way to tell me that I shouldn't listen to what people say about the subject matter, that she and her husband think the book is beautifully written. And he is a lawyer. She told me that you are one of the most important living writers, not just in America, but the entire world. What do you think of that?"

"It's very nice."

"Oh, I love you, my darling. You are my

darling boy, and whatever you do is right. I only wish Daddy was well enough to enjoy all your fame."

"It might have distressed him some, you know."

"He always defended you, always."

"If so, it couldn't have been easy for him."

"But he defended you."

"Good."

"When you were beginning, he was unhappy about some of the things you wrote—involving Cousin Sidney and the friends he had. He wasn't used to it, so he made mistakes. I would never dare to say it to him or he would chop my head off, but I can say it to you: your father was a doer, your father had a mission in life for which everybody loved and respected him, but sometimes, I know it, in his excitement to do right he mistakenly did the wrong thing. But whether you realize it or not, you made him understand. This is true. Behind your back he repeated the very words you used, even if with you he got upset sometimes and argued. That was just a habit. From being your father. But to other people he was behind you like a wall until the day he got sick." He could hear her voice beginning to weaken again. "Of course, you know and I know, once

94

he got into the wheelchair he was unfortunately a different person."

"What is it, Ma?"

"Oh, just everything at once."

"You mean Laura?" He had finally told her—weeks after leaving Bank Street—that he and Laura were no longer together. He had waited until she was over the immediate shock of having a husband move into a nursing home from which he would never return to live with her. One thing at a time, he had thought, though as it turned out, to her it was still everything at once. Of course, it was just as well that his father wasn't in any shape to get the news; all of them, including Laura, agreed he needn't know, especially as in the past, each time Zuckerman left a wife, his father brooded and suffered and grieved, and then, utterly cast down, got on the phone in the middle of the night to apologize to the "poor girl" for his son. There had been scenes about those calls, scenes that summoned up the worst of the son's adolescence.

"You're sure she's all right?" his mother asked.

"She's fine. She's got her work. You don't have to worry about Laura."

"And you'll get divorced, Nathan? Again?"

"Ma, I'm sorry for everyone that I'm compiling such a bad marital record. On dark days I too put myself down for not being an ideal member of my sex. But I just don't have the aptitude for a binding, sentimental attachment to one woman for life. I lose interest and I have to go. Maybe my aptitude is for changing partners—one lovely new woman every five years. Try to see it that way. They're all wonderful, beautiful, devoted girls, you know. There's that to be said for me. I don't bring anything home but the best."

"But I never said you had a bad record— oh, my darling, not me, never, never, never in a million years. You are my son and whatever you decide is right. However you live is right. As long as you know what you're doing."

"I do."

"And as long as you know that it is right."

"It is."

"Then we are behind you. We have been behind you from the very beginning. As Daddy always says, What is a family if they don't stick together?"

Needless to say, he wasn't the best person to ask.

* * *

Dear Mr. Zuckerman:

I read my first erotic book seven years ago when I was thirteen. Then there was a lapse in sexy (and emotionally stimulating) reading as I had the real thing (seven years with the same putz). When that ended last winter it was back to books to forget, to remember, to escape. It was heavy for a while, so I read your book for a laugh. And now I feel as if I'm in love. Well, maybe not love but something as intense. Mr. Zuckerman (dare I call you Nathan?), you are just a definite up emotionally for me—as well as an excellent way to increase my vocabulary. Call me crazy (my friends call me Crazy Julia), call me a literary groupie, but you are truly getting through. You are as therapeutic as my shrink—and only eight ninety-five per session. In these times when a lot of what people communicate to each other is nothing but grief, guilt, hate, and the like, I thought I'd express my gratitude, appreciation, and love for you, your great wit, your fine mind, and everything you stand for.

Oh yes, and one last motive for writing you. Would you consider doing something as impulsive as accompanying me to Europe, say during semester break? I'm somewhat familiar with Switzerland (I have a secret numbered account in the largest Swiss bank) and would love to turn you on to some of the most surreal and moving experiences to be had in that country. We can visit the house in which Thomas Mann spent his last years. His widow and son still live there, in a town called Kilchberg in the canton of Zurich. We can visit the famous chocolate factories, the sound Swiss banking institutions, the mountains, the lakes, the waterfall at which Sherlock Holmes met his destiny—need I go on?

> Not-so-crazy Julia
> Numbered Acc't 776043

Dear Julia:

I am not so crazy either and will have to say no to your invitation. I'm sure you are a completely harmless person, but these are strange times, in America if not Switzerland. I wish I could be friendlier, since you sound friendly and affectionate yourself, not to mention playful and rich. But I'm afraid you'll have to go to the chocolate factories without me.

> Yours,
> Nathan Zuckerman
> Bankers Trust 4863589

Dear Nathan,

I was so sad to leave without saying goodbye. But when Fate changes horses the rider
is carried along.

But this was a real letter, from someone he
knew. Signed "C." He found the envelope in
his wastebasket. It had been mailed several
days earlier in Havana.

Dear Nathan,

I was so sad to leave without saying goodbye. But when Fate changes horses the rider
is carried along. And so I am here. Mary had
always wanted us to meet, and I shall always
feel that my life has been enriched by the
moment—however brief—of knowing you.

Vague memories, nothing but memories.

C.

"Vague memories, nothing but memories"
was Yeats. "Fate changes horses" was Byron.
Otherwise, he thought uncharitably, it looked
to be the form letter. Even the intimate "C."
That stood for Caesara O'Shea, keeper of the
screen's softest, most inviting lilt, of a lan-
guishing air so sad and so seductive that a
Warner Brothers wit had accounted for the

box-office magic thus: "All the sorrow of her race and then those splendid tits." Two weeks earlier Caesara had come to New York from her home in Connemara, and on the phone Zuckerman had been summoned by his agent to be her dinner partner. More *Carnovsky* booty. She had asked specifically for him.

"You'll know most of the people," said André.

"And Caesara you should know," Mary told him. "It's about time."

"Why?" asked Zuckerman.

"Oh, Nathan," said Mary, "don't look down your nose because she's a sex symbol to the hordes. So are you to the hordes, in case you haven't heard."

"Don't be intimidated by the beauty," said André. "Or the press. Everybody gets nasty or shy, and she's nobody to be afraid of. She's a very unassuming, gentle, and intelligent woman. When she's in Ireland all she does is cook and garden and sit at night and read in front of the fire. In New York she's content to walk in the park or just go out to a movie."

"And she's had terrible luck with men," said Mary, "men I'd like to murder, really. Listen to me about you and women, Nathan, because you're as bad as she is. I've watched you mismated three times now. You married the fey elfin dancer who you could crush with one finger, you had the neurotic society girl betraying her class, and as far as I could tell, this last one was actually a certified public saint. Frankly, how you picked that Mother Superior I'll never know. But then there's a little Mother Superior in you too, isn't there? Or maybe that's part of the act. Keeping the Kike at Bay. More Goyish than the Puritan Fathers."

"Right to the heart of my mystery. Can't fool Mary."

"I don't think you fool yourself. For God's sake, come out from behind all that disgusting highbrow disapproval of the fallen people having fun. What's the sense of it after that book? You've thrown all that professor-shit precisely where it belongs—now enjoy a real man's life. And this time with a certified *woman*. Do you really not know what you're getting in Caesara O'Shea? Aside from the most beautiful thing in creation? Dignity, Nathan. Bravery. Strength. Poetry. My God, it's the very heart of Ireland you're getting!"

"Mary, I read the movie magazines too. From the sound of it, her grandfather cut the turf to warm the hut of Mary Magdalene. I may be a comedown from all that."

"Nathan," said André, "I promise you, she'll be as unsure of herself as you are."

"Who isn't," replied Zuckerman, "aside from Mary and Muhammad Ali?"

"He means," said Mary, "that you can be yourself with her."

"And who's that?"

"You'll come up with something," André assured him.

Her gown was a spectacular composition of flame-colored veils and painted wooden beads and cockatoo feathers; her hair hung in a heavy black braid down her back; and her eyes were her eyes. Serving herself the haddock mousse at dinner, she dropped a bit on the floor, making it easier for him to look directly into the celebrated Irish eyes and say things that made sense. Easier until he realized that maybe that was why she'd dropped it. Every time he turned her way, there was that face from those movies.

Not until after dinner, when they were able to move away from the other guests, and from the presumptuous intimacy of place cards inches apart, could they manage to speak intimately. It lasted only five minutes, but did not lack for fervor on either side. They had both read Ellmann's biography of Joyce and, from the sound of it, had never dared to confess the depths of their admiration for the book to anyone before; from the hushed tones, you might have thought that to do so was a criminal offense. Zuckerman revealed that he had once met Professor Ellmann up at Yale. They had actually met at a literary ceremony in New York where each had been awarded a prize, but he didn't want to appear to be trying to impress, given how hard he was trying.

His meeting Ellmann did the trick. He couldn't have come off better had it been Joyce himself. Zuckerman's temples were damp with perspiration, and Caesara had two hands drawn emotionally to her breasts. It was then that he asked if he could see her home later. She whispered yes, twice, mistily, then sailed in her veils across the room—she didn't want to appear oblivious to all the other guests she had been utterly oblivious to. So she put it.

Unsure of herself? A case could be made against that.

On the street, while Zuckerman waved to

attract a cab a block away, a limousine pulled up. "Take me home in this?" Caesara asked.

Curled down beside him in the back seat, she explained that she could call day or night from Ireland and Mary was there to buck her up and tell her whom to hate and revile. He said he got much the same service in New York. She told him about all that the Schevitzes had done for her three children, and he told her about convalescing at their Southampton guest house after having nearly died of a burst appendix. He knew it sounded as though he had almost died of wounds incurred at Byron's side during the struggle for Greek independence, but talking to Caesara O'Shea in the velvety back seat of a dark limousine, you came out sounding a little like Caesara O'Shea in the velvety back seat of a dark limousine. Appendicitis as a passionate, poetic drama. He heard himself being awfully sensitive about the "slant of light" on the Southampton beach during his convalescent morning walks. On and on about the slant of light, when, according to an item in that day's paper, a certain scene in his book was considered responsible for the fifty percent increase in the sale of black silk underwear at smart New York department stores.

You'll come up with something, André had said. And this was it: the slant of light and my operation.

He asked whom she was named for, if anyone. Who was Caesara the First?

In the softest voice imaginable, she told him. "...for a Hebrew woman, the niece of Noah. She sought refuge in Ireland from the universal flood. My people," she said, her white hand to her white throat, "were the first to be interred there. The first of the Irish ghosts."

"You believe in ghosts?" And why not? What better question to ask? How the Movement should respond if Nixon mines Haiphong harbor? Haven't you been over that enough with Laura? Just look at her.

"Let's say the ghosts believe in me," she replied.

"I can understand why they would," said Zuckerman. And why not? Fun was fun. A real man's life.

Still, he made no attempt to embrace her, neither while she was curled girlishly in the back seat feeding him her gentle, harmless, hypnotic blarney, nor when she stood nobly before him at the doorway of the Pierre, a woman nearly his height, with her black braid and her heavy gold earrings and her gown of veils and beads and feathers, looking in all like the pagan goddess they made the sacrifices for in a movie of hers he'd seen at college. Perhaps he might have drawn her to him had he not noticed, on entering the car, a copy of *Carnovsky* lying on the seat beside the driver. The mustached young man must have been reading to pass the time while Miss O'Shea was at dinner. A hip Smilin' Jack in sunglasses and full livery, his nose in Zuckerman's book. No, he wasn't about to impersonate his own hungering hero for the further entertainment of the fans.

Under the lights of the hotel portico, with Smilin' Jack watching sideways from the car, he settled for shaking her hand. Mustn't confuse the driver about the hypothetical nature of fiction. Important to have that straight for the seminars back at the garage.

Zuckerman felt precisely the highbrow fool that Mary Schevitz had him down for. "After all you've been through," he heard himself telling her, "you must be a little suspicious of men."

With her free hand, she drew her silk shawl to her throat. "On the contrary," she assured him, "I admire men. I wish I could have been one."

"That seems an unlikely wish coming from you."

"If I were a man, I could have protected my mother. I could have stood up for her against my father. He drank whiskey and he beat her."

To which Zuckerman could only think to reply, "Good night, Caesara." He kissed her lightly. Staggering to see that face coming up at his. It was like kissing a billboard.

He watched her disappear into the hotel. If only he *were* Carnovsky. Instead, he would go home and write it all down. Instead of having Caesara, he would have his notes.

"Look—" he called, rushing after her into the lobby.

She turned and smiled. "I thought you were hurrying away to see Professor Ellmann."

"I have a proposal. Suppose we cut the crap, as best we can, and have a nightcap."

"Both would be nice."

"Where shall we try it?"

"Why not where all the writers go."

"The New York Public Library? At this hour?"

She was close to him now, on his arm, heading back out the door to where the car was still waiting. The driver knew more than Zuckerman did about Zuckerman. Or about the lure of Miss O'Shea.

"No," she said, "that place they all love so on Second Avenue."

"Elaine's? Oh, I may not be the best person to show you Elaine's. The time I was there with my wife"—he had gone for dinner one evening with Laura, to see what it was all about—"we were seated as close to the lavatory as was possible without actually having the hand-towel concession. You're better off going with Salinger when he gets to town."

"Salinger, Nathan, won't be seen anywhere but El Morocco."

Couples filled the doorway waiting to get in, customers were lined up four deep at the bar waiting for a table, but this time the Zuckerman party was seated with a flourish of the manager's arms, and so far from the toilet that had he needed it in a hurry he might have been at a serious disadvantage.

"Your star has risen," whispered Caesara.

Everyone looked at her while she pretended that they were still talking alone in the car. "People in line out on the street. You'd think it was a Sadean brothel," she
108

said, "instead of just somewhere where they stir up the mud. How I hate these places."

"You do? Why did we come, then?"

"I thought it would be interesting watching you hate it too."

"Hate this? To me it's a great night out."

"I see that by the grinding jaws."

"Sitting here with you," Zuckerman told her, "I can feel my face actually blurring out. I feel like the out-of-focus signpost in a news photo of a head-on collision. Does this happen wherever you go?"

"No, not in the rain in Connemara."

Though they hadn't yet ordered, a waiter arrived with champagne. It was from a smiling gentleman at a corner table.

"For you?" Zuckerman asked Caesara, "or me?" and meanwhile rose half out of his chair to acknowledge the generosity.

"Either way," said Caesara, "you'd better go over—they can turn on you if you don't."

Zuckerman crossed between the tables to shake his hand: a happy, heavyset man, deeply tanned, who introduced the deeply tanned woman with him as his wife.

"Kind of you," said Zuckerman.

"My pleasure. I just want to tell you what a great job you've done with Miss O'Shea."

"Thank you."

"She only has to come on in that dress and she's got the room in the palm of her hand. She looks great. She's still got it. The tragic empress of sex. After all this time. You've done a wonderful job with her."

"Who?" asked Caesara, when Zuckerman returned.

"You."

"What were you talking about?"

"The great job I've done with you. I'm either your hairdresser or your agent."

The waiter uncorked the champagne and they raised their glasses to the corner table. "Now tell me, Nathan, who are the other famous people, aside from yourself? Who's that famous person?"

He knew she knew—everybody in the world knew—but they might as well start having a good time. It's why they were there instead of at the Public Library.

"That," he said, "is a novelist. The establishment roughneck."

"And the man drinking with him?"

"That's a tough journalist with a tender heart. The novelist's loyal second, O'Platitudo."

"Ah, I knew," said Caesara, with the lilt,

"I knew there would be more to Zuckerman than nice manners and clean shoes. Go on."

"That is the *auteur,* the half-wits' intellectual. The guileless girl is his leading lady, the intellectuals' half-wit. That's the editor, the Gentiles' Jew, and that man who is looking at you devouringly is the Mayor of New York, the Jews' Gentile."

"And I had better tell you," said Caesara, "in case he makes a scene, the man at the table behind him, looking furtively at you, is the father of my last child."

"Is it really?"

"I know him by the sinking of my stomach."

"Why? How is he looking at *you?*"

"He isn't. He won't. I was his 'woman.' I gave myself to him and he'll never forgive me for it. He's not merely a monster, he's a great moralist too. Son of a sainted peasant mother who can't thank Jesus enough for all her suffering. I conceived a child by him and refused to allow him to acknowledge it. He waited outside the delivery room with a lawyer. He had papers demanding that the child bear his family's honored name. I would rather have strangled it in the crib. They had to call the police to get him to stop shouting and throw him out. All in the *Los Angeles Times.*"

"I didn't recognize him with the heavy glasses and the banker's suit. The Latin life force."

She corrected him. "The Latin shit. The Latin devious lunatic and liar."

"How did you get involved with him?"

"How do I get involved with the devious lunatics and liars? I work with the he-men in the movies, that's how. Lonely on location, in some ghastly hotel, in some strange place where you can't speak the language—in this case, from my window the view was of two garbage cans and three rats crawling around. Then it starts to rain, and you wait on call for days, and if the he-man wants to charm you and see that you have a good time, and if you don't want to sit reading in your room for sixteen hours a day, and if you want somebody to have dinner with in this ghastly provincial hotel..."

"You could have gotten rid of the child."

"I could have. I could have gotten rid of three children by now. But I wasn't raised to get rid of children. I was raised to be their mother. Either that or a nun. Irish girls aren't raised for any of this."

"You seem to the world to do all right."

"So do you. This fame is a very crude thing,

Nathan. You have to have more insolence than I do to pull it off. You have to be one of the great devious lunatics for that."

"You never like to see your face on all the posters?"

"When I was twenty, I did. You can't imagine all the pleasure I got at twenty just looking in the mirror. I used to look at myself and think that it wasn't possible that somebody should have such a perfect face."

"And now?"

"I'm a little tired of my face. I'm a little tired of what it seems to do to men."

"What is that?"

"Well, it gets them to interviewing me like this, doesn't it? They treat me like a sacred object. Everyone is terrified to lay a finger on me. Probably even the author of *Carnovsky*."

"But there must be those who can't wait to lay a finger on you just because you are a sacred object."

"True. And my children are their offspring. First they sleep with your image, and after they've had that, they sleep with your makeup girl. As soon as it gets through to them that your you isn't the world's you, it's a grave disappointment to the poor fellows. I understand. How often can you get a thrill out of

113

deflowering the kneeling nineteen-year-old
novice of that touching first film, when she's
thirty-five and the mother of three? Oh, the
truth is that I'm really not childish enough
any longer. It was exciting at twenty, but I
don't see much point to it now. Do you? I may
have reached the end of my wonderful future.
I don't even enjoy anymore observing the de-
spicable absurdities. It was a bad idea, coming here. My bad idea. We should go. Unless
you're enjoying yourself too much."

"Oh, being here has delighted me enough
already."

"I should say hello to my child's father.
Before we go. Shouldn't I?"

"I don't know how those things work."

"Do you think all present are waiting to
see if I can do it?"

"I suppose it's the sort of thing some of
them might wait up for."

The confidence so dazzling to him at the
Schevitzes' had all but disappeared; she looked
less certain of herself now than any of the
young models waiting out on the sidewalk
with their boyfriends to get in and catch a
glimpse of the likes of Caesara O'Shea. Still,
she got up and walked across the restaurant
to say hello to her child's father, while Zuck-

erman remained behind and sipped the champagne intended for her hairdresser. He admired that walk. Under the gaze of all those stargazers it was a true dramatic achievement. He admired the whole savory mixture, sauce and stew: the self-satirizing blarney, the deep-rooted vanity, the level-headed hatred, the playfulness, the gameness, the recklessness, the cleverness. And the relentless beauty. And the charm. And the eyes. Yes, enough to keep a man on his toes and away from his work for a lifetime."

On the way out he asked, "How was he?"

"Very cold. Very withdrawn. Very polite. He falls back on the perfidious courtliness. Out of his depth, it's either that or the cruelty. Besides, it's not only the new young mistress he's with; there's also Jessica, Our Sacred Virgin of Radcliffe College. Daughter of the first lucky masochist who made a film in his arms. The innocent child isn't supposed to know yet what a twisted, disgusting, maggoty creature Father is."

When they were back in the limousine she drew herself up straight inside the flame-colored veils and looked out the window.

"How did you get into all this?" he asked

as they drove along. "If you were raised to be a nun or a mother."

"'All this,' meaning what?" she said sharply. "Show biz? Masochism? Whoredom? How did I get into all this? You sound like a man in bed with a prostitute."

"Another twisted, disgusting, maggoty creature."

"Oh, Nathan, I'm sorry." She gripped his arm and held it as though they had been together all their lives. "Oh, I got into all this as innocently as any girl could. Playing Anne Frank at the Gate Theatre. I was nineteen years old. I had half of Dublin in tears."

"I didn't know that," said Zuckerman.

They were back at the Pierre. "Would you like to come up? Oh, of course you would," said Caesara. No false modesty about her magic, but on the other hand, no swagger either: a fact was a fact. He followed her into the lobby, his face blurring out again as hers now caught the gaze of people leaving the hotel. He was thinking of Caesara starting at nineteen as the enchanting Anne Frank, and of the photographs of film stars like the enchanting Caesara which Anne Frank pinned up beside that attic bed. That Anne Frank should come to him in this guise. That he should meet her at his agent's house, in a dress of veils and beads and cockatoo feathers. That he should take her to Elaine's to be gaped at. That she should invite him up to her penthouse suite. Yes, he thought, life has its own flippant ideas about how to handle serious fellows like Zuckerman. All you have to do is wait and it teaches you all there is to know about the art of mockery.

The first thing he saw in her drawing room was a pile of brand-new books on the dresser; three were by him—paperback copies of *Higher Education, Mixed Emotions,* and *Reversed Intentions.* Beside the books was a vase holding two dozen yellow roses. He wondered who they were from, and when she put down her shawl and went off to the bathroom he sidled over to the dresser and read the card. "To my Irish rose, Love and love and love, F." When she came back into the room, he was in the wing chair that looked across the park to the towers on Central Park West, leafing through the book that had been open on the table beside the chair. It was by Søren Kierkegaard, of all people. Called *The Crisis in the Life of an Actress.*

"And what is the crisis in the life of an actress?" he asked.

She made a sad face and dropped into the settee across from him. "Getting older."

"According to Kierkegaard or according to you?"

"Both of us." She reached across and he handed her the book. She flipped through to find the right page. "'When,'" she read, "'she'—the actress—'is only thirty years old she is essentially passé.'"

"In Denmark maybe, in 1850. I wouldn't take it to heart if I were you. Why are you reading this?"

He wondered if it had come from "F." along with the roses.

"Why shouldn't I?" asked Caesara.

"No reason. I suppose everybody should. What else have you underlined?"

"What everybody underlines," she said. "Everything that says 'me.'"

"May I see?" He leaned over to take the book back.

"Would you like a drink?" said Caesara.

"No, thanks. I'd like to see the book."

"You can look across the park from here up to where Mike Nichols lives. That's his triplex where the lights are. Do you know him?"

"Caesara, everybody knows Mike Nichols,"

Zuckerman said. "Knowing Mike Nichols is considered nothing in this town. Come on, let me see the book. I never heard of it before."

"You're making fun of me," she said. "For leaving Kierkegaard out to impress you. But I also left your books out to impress you."

"Come on, let me see what interests you so much."

Finally she passed it back to him. "Well, *I* want a drink," she said, and got up and poured herself some wine from an open bottle near the flowers. Lafite-Rothschild—also from F.? "I should have known I was to be graded."

"'And she,'" Zuckerman read aloud, "'who as a woman is sensitive regarding her name— as only a woman is sensitive—she knows that her name is on everyone's lips, even when they wipe their mouths with their handkerchiefs!' Do you know that?"

"I know that, I know things even less enchanting than that, needless to say."

"Say it anyway."

"No need. Except it isn't quite what my mother had in mind when she took me down from Dublin in my Peter Pan collar to audition for my scholarship at RADA."

The phone rang, but she ignored it. F.? or G.? or H.?

119

"'She knows that she is the subject of everyone's admiring conversation,'" Zuckerman read to her, "'including those who are in the utmost distress for something to chatter about. She lives on in this way year after year. That seems just splendid; it looks as though that would really be something. But if in a higher sense she had to live on the rich nourishment of their admiration, take encouragement from it, receive strength and inspiration for renewed exertions—and since even the most highly talented person, and particularly a woman, can become despondent in a weak moment for want of some expression of genuine appreciation—at such a time she will really feel what she has doubtless realized often enough, just how fatuous all this is, and what a mistake it is to envy her this burdensome splendor.' The hardships," said Zuckerman, "of the idolized woman." He began turning pages again, looking for her markings.

"You're welcome to borrow it, Nathan. Of course you're also welcome to stay here and just proceed right on through."

Zuckerman laughed. "And what will you do?"

"What I always do when I invite a man to

my room and he sits down and starts reading. I'll throw myself from the window."

"Your problem is this taste of yours, Caesara. If you just had Harold Robbins around, like the other actresses, it would be easier to pay attention to you."

"I thought I would impress you with my brains and instead it's Kierkegaard's brain you're impressed with."

"There's always that danger," he said.

This time, when the phone began ringing, she lifted the receiver, then quickly put it back down. Then she picked it up again and dialed the hotel operator. "Please, no more calls until noon...Fine. I know. I *know*. I have the message. Please, I'd just appreciate it if you'd do as I say. I have all the messages, *thank you.*"

"Would you like me to leave?" asked Zuckerman.

"Would you like to?"

"Of course not."

"Okay," she said, "where are we? Oh. You tell me. What is the crisis in the life of a writer? What obstacles must *he* overcome in his relation to the public?"

"First, their indifference; then, when he's lucky, their attention. It's your profession

121

having people look you over, but I can't get used to the gaping. I prefer my exhibitionism at several removes."

"Mary says you won't even go out of the house anymore."

"Tell Mary I never went out of the house much before. Look, I didn't go into this line of work so as to stir the masses to a frenzy."

"What then?"

"What I set out to do? Oh, I was a good boy too in my Peter Pan collar, and believed everything Aristotle taught me about literature. Tragedy exhausts pity and fear by arousing those emotions to the utmost, and comedy promotes a carefree, lighthearted state of mind in the audience by showing them that it would be absurd to take seriously the action being imitated. Well, Aristotle let me down. He didn't mention anything about the theater of the ridiculous in which I am now a leading character—because of literature."

"Oh, it's not all ridiculous. It seems that way to you only because you're so intensity-afflicted."

"And whose epithet is that? Mary's too?"

"No, mine. I've got the same disease."

"In that dress?"

"In this dress. Don't be fooled by the dress."
The phone began its ringing again.

"Seems like he's slipped past the guard," said Zuckerman and opened the book to pass the time while she decided whether or not to answer. *So now for the metamorphosis,* he read. *This actress was constituted by feminine youthfulness, though not in the usual sense of the term. What is normally called youthfulness falls prey to the years; for the grip of time may be most loving and careful, but it seizes everything finite just the same. But in this actress there has been an essential genius which corresponds to the very idea: feminine youthfulness. This is an idea, and an idea is something quite different—*

"Is the point you're making, reading in my little book, that you are nothing like the notorious character in your own? Or," she asked, once the phone had stopped ringing, "is it that I'm not desirable?"

"To the contrary," said Zuckerman. "Your allure is staggering and you can't imagine how depraved I am."

"Then borrow the book and read it at home."

* * *

He came down into the deserted lobby at close to four, carrying the Kierkegaard. The moment he stepped out of the revolving door, Caesara's limousine pulled up in front of the hotel, and there was Caesara's driver, the dude who'd been reading *Carnovsky,* saluting him through the open window. "Drop you somewhere, Mr. Zuckerman?"

This too? Had he been instructed to wait until four? Or all night if need be? Caesara had awakened Zuckerman and said, "I'd rather face the dawn alone, I think." "Painters coming early?" "No. But all the brushing of teeth and flushing of toilets is more than I'm ready for." Sweet surprise. First faint touch of the girl in the Peter Pan collar. He had to admit he was feeling swamped himself.

"Sure," he told her driver. "You can take me home."

"Hop in." But he didn't hop out to open the door as he did when Miss O'Shea was along. Well, thought Zuckerman, maybe he's finished the book.

They drove slowly up Madison, Zuckerman reading her Kierkegaard under the lamp in the soft back seat... *She knows that her name is on everyone's lips, even when they wipe their mouths with their handkerchiefs!* He didn't know if it was just the excitement of a new woman, the thrill of all that unknownness— and of all that glamour—or if it could possibly be that in just eight hours he had fallen in love, but he devoured the paragraph as though she *had* inspired it. He couldn't believe his luck. And it didn't seem such a misfortune, either. "No, not entirely ridiculous. Much to be said for stirring the masses, if that's what stirred you too. I'm not going to sneer at how I got here." To her, and silently, he said this, then wiped his mouth, a little stupefied. All from literature. Imagine that. He would not like to have to tell Dr. Leavis, but he didn't feel the least sacrilegious.

When they got to his house, the driver refused his ten dollars. "No, no, Mr. Z. My privilege." Then he took a business card from his billfold and handed it out the window. "If we can ever put your mind at ease, sir," and sped away while Zuckerman stepped under the streetlight to read the card:

RATE SCHEDULE

Per Hour

Armed Driver and Limousine 27.50
Unarmed Driver and Armed Escort
    with Limousine 32.50

Armed Driver and Armed Escort
with Limousine 36.00
Additional Armed Escorts 14.50
Five Hour Minimum
Major Credit Cards Honoured
(212) 555–8830

He read for the rest of the night—her
book—and then at nine he phoned the hotel
and was reminded that Miss O'Shea wasn't
taking calls until noon. He left his name,
wondering what he would do with himself
and his exultation until they met at two for
their walk through the park—she'd said it
would be happiness enough just doing that.
He couldn't look at *The Crisis in the Life of
an Actress* again, or the two essays on drama
that filled out the little volume. He'd been
through them all twice already—the second
time at six a.m., making notes in the journal
he kept for his reading. He couldn't stop
thinking about her, but that was an improvement over trying to take in what people were
thinking, saying, and writing about him—
there is such a thing as self-satiation. "You
would imagine," he said to the empty book-
shelves when he came in, "that after wine at
dinner, champagne at Elaine's, and inter-

course with Caesara, I could put the homework off until morning and get some rest."
But at least sitting at his desk with a pen and
a pad and a book, he had felt a little less goofy
than lying in bed with her name on his lips
like the rest of the fans. It didn't, of course,
feel anything like a good night's work; he
hadn't felt the excitement of working straight
through the night since his last weeks finishing *Carnovsky*. Nor could he lay claim to some
lively new idea about what book to write next.
All lively new ideas were packed away like
the volumes in the eighty-one cartons. But at
least he'd been able to focus on something
other than himself being stuffed to bursting
at the trough of inanities. He was bursting
now with her.

He called the Pierre, couldn't get through,
and then didn't know what to do with himself.
Begin to unpack the half ton of books, that's
what! Bank Street is over! Laura is over! Uncarton all the boxed-in brains! Then uncarton
your own!

But he had an even better idea. André's
tailor! Hold the books and buy a suit! For
when we fly to Venice—for checking in at
the Cipriani! (Caesara had allowed, as he was
leaving, that the only hotel in the world

where she truly enjoyed awakening in the morning was the Cipriani.)

In his wallet he found André's tailor's card, his shirtmaker's card, his wine merchant's card, and his Jaguar dealer's card; these had been ceremoniously presented to Zuckerman over lunch at the Oak Room the day André had completed the sale to Paramount of the film rights to *Carnovsky,* bringing Zuckerman's income for 1969 to just over a million, or approximately nine hundred and eighty-five thousand dollars more than he had previously earned in any year of his life. Placing André's cards in his wallet, Zuckerman had withdrawn a card he had prepared the night before for André and handed it across to him—a large index card on which he had typed a line from the letters of Henry James. *All this is far from being life as I feel it, as I see it, as I know it, as I wish to know it.* But his agent was neither edified nor amused. "The world is yours, Nathan, don't hide from it behind Henry James. It's bad enough that that's what he hid behind. Go see Mr. White, tell him who sent you, and get him to fit you out the way he does Governor Rockefeller. It's time to stop looking like some kid at Harvard and assume your role in history."

128

Well, at Mr. White's that morning—waiting for Caesara to get up—he ordered six suits. If you're in a sweat over one, why *not* six? But why in a sweat? He had the dough. All he needed now was the calling.

On which side did he dress? asked Mr. White. It took a moment to fathom the meaning, and then to realize that he didn't know. If *Carnovsky* was any indication, he had for thirty-six years given more thought than most to the fate of his genitals, but whither they inclined while he went about the day's uncarnal business, he had no idea.

"Neither, really," he said.

"Thank you, sir," said Mr. White, and made a note.

On the new fly he was to have buttons. As he remembered, it was a big day in a little boy's life when he was old enough to be trusted not to get himself caught in a zipper and so bid farewell to the buttoned-up fly. But when Mr. White, an Englishman of impeccable grooming and manners, wondered aloud if Mr. Zuckerman might not prefer to change over to buttons, Zuckerman caught the tone and, mopping his face, replied, "Oh, absolutely." Whatever the Governor has, he thought. And Dean Acheson. His picture also

129

hung among the notables on Mr. White's paneled walls.

When the taking of the measurements was over, Mr. White and an elderly assistant helped Zuckerman back into his jacket without giving any sign that they were handling rags. Even the assistant was dressed for a board meeting of A.T.&T.

Here, as though retiring to the rare-book room at the Bodleian, the three turned to where the bolts of cloth were stored. Fabrics that would serve Mr. Zuckerman for the city and his club; for the country and his weekends; for the theater, for the opera, for dining out. Each was removed from its shelf by the assistant so that Mr. Zuckerman might appreciate the cloth between his fingers. In North America, he was told, with its extremes of climate, a dozen suits would be best to cover every contingency, but Mr. Zuckerman stuck at six. He was drenched already.

Then the linings. Lavender for the gray suit. Gold for the tan suit. A daring floral pattern for the country twill... Then the styling. Two-piece or three-piece? Double-breasted or single-breasted? Two-button front or three-button front? Lapels this wide or this wide? Center vents or side vents? The inside coat pocket—one or two, and how deep? Back trouser pockets—button on the left or the right? And will you be wearing suspenders, sir?

Would he, at the Cipriani, for checking in?

They were attending to the styling of his trousers—Mr. White, most respectfully, making his case for a modest flare at the cuff of the twill—when Zuckerman saw that finally it was noon. Urgent phone call, he announced. "Of course, sir," and he was left to himself, amid the bolts of cloth, to dial the Pierre.

But she was gone. Checked out. Any message for Mr. Zuckerman? None. Had she received *his* message? She had. But where had she gone? The desk had no idea—though suddenly Zuckerman did. To move in with André and Mary! She'd left the hotel to shake the unwanted suitor. She had made her choice and it was him!

He was wrong. It was the other guy.

"*Nathan*," said Mary Schevitz. "I've been trying all morning to reach *you*."

"I'm at the tailor's, Mary, suiting up for every contingency. Where is she if she's not with you two?"

"Nathan, you must understand—she left

131

in tears. I've never seen her so distraught. It killed *me*. She said, 'Nathan Zuckerman is the best thing that's happened to me in a year.'"

"So where is she then? Why did she go?"

"She flew to Mexico City. She's flying from there to Havana. Nathan dear, I didn't know anything. Nobody's known anything. It's the best-kept secret in the world. She only told me to try to explain to me how badly she felt about you."

"Told you what?"

"She's been having an affair. Since March. With Fidel Castro. Nathan, you mustn't tell anyone. She wants to end it with him, she knows there's no future there. She's sorry it ever began. But he's a man who won't take no for an answer."

"As the world knows."

"He had his UN Ambassador phoning her every five minutes since she arrived. And this morning the Ambassador came to the hotel and insisted on taking her to breakfast. And then she called me to say she was going, that she had to. Oh, Nathan, I do feel responsible."

"Don't, Mary. Kennedy couldn't stop him, Johnson couldn't stop him, Nixon won't stop him. So how can you? Or I?"

"And you looked so charming together. Have you seen the *Post?*"

"I haven't been out of the fitting room."

"Well, it's in Leonard Lyons, about the two of you at Elaine's."

Later that day his mother phoned to tell him that it had been on the air as well; in fact, she was phoning to find out if it could possibly be true that he had flown to Ireland, without even calling her to say goodbye.

"Of course I would have called," he assured her.

"Then you're not going."

"No."

"Bea Wirth phoned me just a minute ago to say that she heard it on the television. Nathan Zuckerman is off to Ireland to stay at the palatial country estate of Caesara O'Shea. It was on Virginia Graham. I didn't even know she was a friend of yours."

"She's not, really."

"I didn't think so. She's so much older than you."

"She's not, but that isn't the point."

"She is, darling. Daddy and I saw Caesara O'Shea years ago already, playing a nun."

"Playing a novice. She was practically a child then."

133

"It never sounded from the papers as though she was a child."

"Well, maybe not."

"But everything is all right? You feel well?"

"I'm fine. How's Dad?"

"He's a little better. I'm not saying that just to make myself feel good, either. Mr. Metz has been going every afternoon now to read him the *Times*. He says Daddy seems to follow perfectly. He can tell by how angry he gets whenever he hears Nixon's name."

"Well, that's terrific, isn't it?"

"But you going away without calling—I told Bea it just couldn't be. Nathan wouldn't dream of going that far without telling me, in case God forbid I had to get hold of him about his father."

"That's true."

"But why did Virginia Graham say you did? And on TV?"

"Someone must have told her an untruth, Ma."

"They did? But why?"

Dear Mr. Zuckerman:

For a number of years I have been planning to film a series of half-hour television shows (in color) to be called "A Day in the Life of..." The format, which is no more than a carbon of the ancient Greek Tragedy, is a recitation of the hour-by-hour activities of a well-known person, and offers an intimate personal look at someone who, in the normal course of events, the audience would not see or meet. My company, Renowned Productions, is fully financed and ready to embark upon its opening show. Briefly, it involves filming one complete day, from breakfast to bedtime, of a celebrity who will excite the interest of millions of onlookers. To achieve one day without dull spots, we will average four days of filming candid unrehearsed material.

I selected you as our first celebrity because I think your day will be as interesting as any I can envision. Also, there is broad public interest in you and your "offstage" life. Everyone, I think, would profit by watching a candid portrayal of you at work and you at play. My guess is that such a production will enhance your career—and mine too.

Please let me know your feelings, and if we agree, I will send a couple of reporters to start the initial research.

> Sincerely,
> Gary Wyman
> President

Dear Mr. Wyman:

I think you underestimate how many days, weeks, and years of filming it would take to achieve "A Day in the Life of..." of me that would be without dull spots. A candid portrayal of my offstage life would probably put millions of viewers to sleep and, far from enhancing your career, destroy it forever. Better start with somebody else. Sorry.

> Sincerely,
> Nathan Zuckerman

Dear Mr. Zuckerman:

I have written a short novel of approximately 50,000 words. It is a romance with college characters and explicit sex but has humor and other interest as well, and an original plot. As in your latest book, the sexual activity is an integral part of the plot, so is essential.

I intended to send it to Playboy Press but have backed down because there could be repercussions. My wife and I are retired, living very happily in a retirement village in Tampa. If the book turned out to be successful and the people here found out that I wrote it, we would lose our friends at once and would probably have to sell our home and leave.

I hate to do nothing about the book because I believe it would be entertaining for readers who like explicit sex and also those who don't mind it as long as there is something worthwhile accompanying it. You are an established author and can publish such a book, as you already have, without worrying about adverse opinion.

Please let me know if I may send you the manuscript, and also the address I should use. Then if you like it, you may wish to buy it outright from me as an investment and publish it under another name than your own.

Sincerely,
Harry Nicholson

The phone.

"All right then," cried Zuckerman, "who is this? You, Nicholson?"

"Right now we are asking for only fifty

thousand. That's because we haven't had to do the job. Kidnapping is an expensive operation. It takes planning, it takes thought, it takes highly trained personnel. If we have to go ahead and get to work, fifty thousand won't begin to cover costs. If I am going to keep my head above water, you won't get out of a kidnapping like this for under three hundred thousand. In a kidnapping like this, with nationwide coverage, we run a tremendous risk and everybody involved has to be compensated accordingly. Not to mention equipment. Not to mention time. But if you want us to go ahead, we will. Hang up on me again and you'll see how fast. My people are poised."

"Poised where, palooka?" For it was still with something like the caricatured voice of a punch-drunk pug that the caller was endeavoring to disguise his own—and threatening to kidnap Zuckerman's mother. "Look," said Zuckerman, "this isn't funny."

"I want fifty thousand bucks in cash. Otherwise we proceed with the full-scale operation and then you will be out three hundred thousand at least. Not to mention the wear and tear on your old lady. Have a heart, Zuck. Haven't you given her enough misery with that book? Don't make it any worse than it already is. Don't make it so that she regrets the day you were born, sonny."

"Look, this is call number three and has by now become a disgusting sadistic psychopathic little joke—"

"Oh, don't you tell me about disgusting jokes! Don't you call me names, you highbrow fuck! You fake! Not after what you do to your family, you heartless bastard—and in the name of Great Art! In my daily life I am a better man than you are a hundred times over, shitface. Everybody who knows me personally knows that. I detest violence. I detest suffering. What goes on in this country today makes me sick. We had a great leader in Robert Kennedy, and that crazy Arab bastard shot him. Robert Kennedy, who could have turned this country around! But what people know me to be as a human being is none of your business. God knows I don't have to prove myself to a faker like you. Right now we are talking strictly money, and it is no more disgusting than when you talk on the phone to the accountant. You have got fifty thousand dollars, I want it. It's as simple as that. I don't know a son in your financial position who would think twice about laying out

139

fifty thousand to spare his mother some terrible tragic experience. Suppose it was cancer, would you think that was a disgusting joke too, would you make her go through that too, rather than dig into the margin account? Christ, you have just got close to another million on the sequel. How much more do you need in one year? The way the world gets the story, you're so pure you hold your nose when you have to handle change from the taxicab. You fraud, you hypocrite! Your talent I can't take away from you, but as a human being exploiting other human beings you haven't got the greatest record, you know, so don't get high and mighty with me. Because if it was my mother, let me tell you, there wouldn't be that much to debate about. I'd act, and fast. But then I would never have gotten her into this to begin with. I wouldn't have the talent for it. I wouldn't have the talent to exploit my family and make them a laughingstock the way you have. I'm not gifted enough to do that."

"So you do this," said Zuckerman, wondering meanwhile what *he* should do. What would Joseph Conrad do? Leo Tolstoy? Anton Chekhov? When first starting out as a young writer in college he was always putting things to himself that way. But that didn't seem much help now. Probably better to ask what Al Capone would do.

"Correct," he was told, "so I do this. But I don't do it with violence and I don't do it where the traffic can't bear the freight. I do research. And given operating expenses, I am by no means exorbitant in my demands. I am not interested in causing suffering. I hate suffering. I have seen enough suffering in my personal life to last forever. All I care about is making a reasonable profit on my investment and the man-hours involved. And to do what I do with responsibility. I assure you, not everybody goes about it the responsible way that I do. Not everybody thinks these things through. They kidnap like madmen, they kidnap like school kids, and that is when the shit hits the fan. My pride won't permit that. My compunctions won't permit that. I try like hell to avoid just that. And I do, when I am met on the other side by a person with compunctions like my own. I've been in this business many years now, and nobody has been hurt yet who wasn't asking for it by being greedy."

"Where did you hear that I just made a million on 'the sequel'?" If only he had a tape recorder. But the little Sony was down on Bank Street in Laura's office. Everything was that he needed.

"I didn't 'hear' it. I don't operate that way. I've got it right in front of me in your file. I'm reading it right now. *Variety,* out Wednesday. 'Independent Bob "Sleepy" Lagoon paid close to a million—'"

"But that is a lie. That is Independent Lagoon puffing himself up without paying a dime. There is no sequel."

Wasn't this the right approach, the one they recommended in the papers? To level with the kidnapper, to take him seriously, to make him your friend and equal?

"That isn't what Mr. Lagoon tells my staff, however. Funny, but I tend to trust my staff on this more than I trust you."

"My good man, Lagoon is promoting himself, period." It's Pepler, he thought. It's Alvin Pepler, the Jewish Marine!

"Haw, haw, haw. Very funny. No less than I expected from the savage satirist of American letters."

"Look, who is this?"

"I want fifty thousand in United States currency. I want it in hundred-dollar bills. Unmarked, please."

"And how would I get you the fifty thousand unmarked dollars?"

"Ah, now we are talking, now we are making some progress. You just go to your bank in Rockefeller Plaza and you get it out. We'll tell you when, at the time. Then you start walking. Easy as that. Doesn't even require a college degree. Put the money in your briefcase, go back out on the street, and just start walking. We take care of everything from there. No police, Nathan. If you smell of police, it'll get ugly. I detest violence. My kids can't watch TV because of the violence. Jack Ruby, Jack Idiot Ruby, has become the patron saint of America! I can hardly live in this country anymore because of the violence. You aren't the only one who is against this stinking war. It's a nightmare, it's a national disgrace. I will do everything in my power to avoid violence. But if I smell police, I am going to feel threatened and I am going to have to act like a threatened man. That means police stinking up Miami Beach and police stinking up New York."

"Friend," said Zuckerman, changing tactics, "too many grade-B movies. The lingo, the laugh, everything. Unoriginal. Unconvincing. Bad art."

"Haw, haw, haw. Could be, Zuck. Haw, haw, haw. Also real life. We'll be in touch to set the hour."

This time it wasn't the novelist who hung up.

3

Oswald, Ruby, et al.

Out of the front windows of his new apartment, Zuckerman could see down to the corner of his street to Frank E. Campbell, the Madison Avenue funeral parlor where they process for disposal the richest, most glamorous, and most celebrated of New York's deceased. On display in the chapel, the morning after Alvin Pepler and the threatening phone calls, lay a gangland figure, Nick "the Prince" Seratelli, who had died the day before from a cerebral hemorrhage—instead of in a spray of bullets—at a spaghetti house downtown. By nine in the morning a few bystanders had already collected around Campbell's doors to identify the entertainers, athletes, politicians, and criminals who would be arriving to get a last look at the Prince. Through the slats of his shutters, Zuckerman watched two mounted cops talking to three armed foot patrolmen guarding the funeral parlor's side door down the way from him on Eighty-first. There would be more out at the main entrance on Madison, and easily a dozen plainclothesmen moseying around the neighborhood. Here was the kind of police protection he had been thinking about all night for his mother.

This was only the third or fourth gala staged at Campbell's since Zuckerman had moved uptown. Ordinary, unnoteworthy funerals occurred every day, however, so that he had almost learned by now to ignore the cluster of mourners and the hearse by the side door across the street when he came out of the house in the morning. It wasn't easy, though, especially on mornings when the sun rolling over the East Side caught them full in the face like so many lucky vacationers on a Caribbean cruise ship; nor was it easy on mornings when the rain drummed down on their umbrellas as they waited for the funeral procession to begin, nor even on gray run-of-the-mill days, when it neither rains nor shines. No weather he'd come across yet made

146

seeing somebody sealed up in a box something he could easily forget.

The caskets were trucked in during the day, unloaded with a forklift, then lowered in the freight elevator to the mortuary basement. Down, and down again, the first test-run. Flowers that had dropped off the wreaths going on to the cemetery or the crematorium were swept up by the uniformed black porter after the cortege bearing the body had moved out of sight. The dead petals the porter didn't get, the city sanitation machine caught among the curbside debris on the following Tuesday or Thursday. As for the dead bodies, they arrived on narrow stretchers, in dark sacks, generally after the streetlights came on. An ambulance, sometimes a station wagon, pulled into Campbell's reserved parking spot and the sack was whisked in through the side door. Over in seconds—yet during his first months uptown, it seemed to Zuckerman that he was always passing by in time to see it. Lights stayed on in the upper stories of the funeral home at all hours. No matter how late he went into the living room to turn off his own lamps, he saw theirs burning. And not because anyone was up reading or couldn't

147

sleep. Lights that kept no one awake, except Zuckerman in his bed, remembering them.

At times, amid the crowd of mourners awaiting the pallbearers and the coffin, somebody would stare across at Zuckerman as he passed by. Because he was Zuckerman, or because he was staring at them? Couldn't tell, but as he preferred not to distract anyone at a time like that with either himself or his book, he learned within only weeks to master the shock of coming upon such a gathering virtually across from his front door the first thing each day, and, as though death left him cold, hurried on about the business of buying the morning paper and his onion roll.

He had been up all night, not only because of the lights burning at Campbell's. He was waiting to see if the kidnapper would call again or if the joke was over. At three a.m. he had nearly reached out from his bed and telephoned Laura. At four he nearly telephoned the police. At six he nearly called Miami Beach. At eight he got up and looked out the front window, and when he saw the cop on horseback outside the funeral home he thought of his father in the nursing home. He had been thinking of his father at three and four and six as well. He often did when he saw the lights burning all night at Campbell's. He was unable to get a song called "Tzena, Tzena" out of his head. They were a great family for whistling while they worked, and "Tzena, Tzena" his father had whistled for years, after putting in a decade with "Bei Mir Bist Du Schoen." "This song," Dr. Zuckerman told his family, "is going to win more hearts to the Jewish cause than anything before in the history of the world." The chiropodist even ran out to get it, maybe the fifth record he had bought in his life. Zuckerman was home for the Christmas vacation of his sophomore year, and "Tzena, Tzena" was played every night before dinner. "This is the song," Dr. Zuckerman said, "that will put the State of Israel on the map." Unfortunately, Nathan was beginning to learn about counterpoint in his humanities course, so when the father made the mistake at dinner of genially asking his older son's musical opinion, he was told that Israel's future would be determined by international power politics and not by feeding Gentiles "Jewish kitsch." Causing Dr. Zuckerman to pound the table: "That is where you are wrong! There is exactly where you fail to understand the feelings of the ordinary man!" They had dis-

149

agreed all that Christmas, not only about the value of "Tzena, Tzena." But by the mid-sixties, when he played for Nathan the Barry Sisters singing the songs from *Fiddler on the Roof,* the struggle was about over. By then the father was in a wheelchair in Miami Beach, the older son a recognized writer long out of school, and after sitting down to listen to the show tunes straight through, Nathan told him they were terrific. "At the Temple," said his mother, "after the services last week, the cantor sang the title song for us. You could have heard a pin drop." Since Dr. Zuckerman's first stroke, he had begun attending Friday-night religious services with Zuckerman's mother. The first time in their lives. So that the rabbi who buried him wouldn't be a total stranger. Not that anybody had to say as much. "These Barry Sisters," his father announced, "and this record are going to do more for the Jews than anything since 'Tzena, Tzena.'" "You could be right," said Nathan. And why not? He was no longer a student in Humanities 2, the damage that he had done the Jewish cause by writing his first book was no longer one of his father's unshakable obsessions, and *Carnovsky* was still three years off.

Instead of calling Laura, the police, or Florida, he used his head and at ten decided to phone André, who would know what to make of these threats. His gallant continental manner, his rippling silver hair, his Old World accent—all had earned him ages ago the mildly derisive *nom de guerre* "the Headwaiter"; but to those he did the business for, rather than those he gave it to, André Schevitz was more estimable than that. In addition to ministering to his international roster of novelists, André looked after the megalomania, alcoholism, satyriasis, and tax tragedies of fifteen world-famous film stars. He flew off at a moment's notice to hold their hands on location, and once every few months made it a point to call on little children around the country with mamas away making sagas in Spain or papas off in Liechtenstein tending to their dummy corporations. During the summer any child all but orphaned because of a domestic cataclysm headlined in the *National Enquirer* wound up spending school vacation with André and Mary in Southampton; on a hot August day it wasn't unusual to see two or three miniature replicas of the cinema's most photographed faces gobbling watermelon at the edge of the Schevitz pool.

Zuckerman's first painful divorce, the one from Betsy nine years earlier, had been painlessly engineered for him at five-and-dime-store rates by André's (and Mrs. Rockefeller's) lawyer; two years back his life had been saved by André's society surgeon; and the scene of his convalescence from the burst appendix and peritonitis had been the Schevitz Southampton guest house: with a Schevitz maid and cook in attendance—and on weekends, his own Laura—he had snoozed on the sun deck, lolled in the pool, and regained the twenty pounds he'd lost during the month in the hospital. And had begun writing *Carnovsky*.

Oh, but those threats, those threats were just more ridiculousness—and he didn't need his agent to remind him. Zuckerman found a fresh composition book and, instead of phoning André, began to record what he could still recall of the previous day's business. Because this *was* his business: not buying and selling, but seeing and believing. Oppressive perhaps from a personal point of view, but from the point of view of business? My God, from the point of view of business, yesterday was wonderful! He should do business like that every day. *Didn't we get your teeth cleaned? Sharp new suits? A dermatologist? Alvin, we are not hardened criminals—we are in show business. We're so worried about you, he tells me, we've decided to pay for a psychiatrist for you. We want you to see Dr. Eisenberg until you have gotten over your neurosis and are yourself again. Absolutely, Schachtman says, I see Dr. Eisenberg, why shouldn't Alvin see Dr. Eisenberg?*

He wrote steadily for over an hour, every irate word of Pepler's deposition, and then, suddenly, broke into a sweat and telephoned André at his office to recount to him the details of the phone calls, right down to the haw, haw, haws.

"To resist all the temptations I strew in your path, this I understand. To fight the way your life is going," said André, capitalizing, for the sake of the satire, on the Mitteleuropa inflections, "to be unable to accept what has happened to you, this I also understand. Even if it is you yourself who has kicked over your traces, what happens when you kick over your traces can take anybody by surprise. Especially a boy with your background. What with Papa telling you to be good, and Mama telling you to be nice, and the University of Chicago training you four years in Advanced

Humanistic Decisions, well, what chance did you ever have to lead a decent life? To take you away to that place at sixteen! It's like stealing a wild little baby baboon from the branches of the trees, feeding him in the kitchen, letting him sleep in your bed and play with the light switch and wear little shirts and pants with pockets, and then, when he is big and hairy and full of himself, giving him his degree in Western Civilization and sending him back to the bush. I can just imagine what an enchanting little baboon you were at the University of Chicago. Pounding the seminar table, writing English on the blackboard, screaming at the class that they had it all wrong—you must have been all over the place. Rather like the Nathan in this abrasive little book."

"What's your point, André? Someone is threatening to kidnap my mother."

"My point is that to turn a jungle baboon into a seminar baboon is a cruel, irreversible process. I understand why you won't ever be happy around the waterhole again. But paranoia is something else. And my point for you, my question to you, is how far are you going to let paranoia take you before it takes you where it goes?"

154

"The question is how far the abrasive little book is going to take *them*."

"Nathan, who are 'they'? Nathan, you must do me a favor and stop going nuts."

"I had three phone calls last night from some madman threatening to kidnap my mother. Nuts it sounds, *but it happened*. What I am now trying to figure out is what to do in response that isn't nuts. I thought a worldly fellow with your admirable cynicism might have had some experience with this sort of thing."

"I can only tell you that I haven't. Among my clients are the richest and best-known stars in the world, but as far as I know, nothing like this has ever 'happened' to any of them."

"Nothing like this ever happened to me, either. That may account for why I sound the way I do."

"I understand that. But you have been sounding this way for some time. You have been sounding this way from the day it began. In all my years of experience with high-strung prima donnas, I have never seen anyone make such a fiasco of fame and fortune. I have seen all sorts of crazy indulgence, but

155

never before indulgence in anything like this. To be chagrined by such good fortune. Why?"

"Because of the madmen who call me on the phone, for one."

"Then don't answer the phone. Don't sit there waiting by the phone, and that takes care of the phone. To take care of the bus, don't ride the bus. And while you're at it, stop eating in those filthy delicatessens. You are a rich man."

"Who says I eat in filthy delicatessens? The *News* or the *Post?*"

"I say so. And isn't it true? You buy greasy takeout chickens at these foul little barbecue holes and you eat them with your hands in that barren apartment. You hide out in Shloimie's Pastrami Haven, pretending to be harmless Mr. Nobody from Nowhere. And by now it is all beginning to lose its eccentric charm, Nathan, and is taking on a decidedly paranoiac aroma. What are you up to, anyway? Are you out to appease the gods? Are you trying to show them up in heaven and over at *Commentary* that you are only a humble, self-effacing yeshiva *bucher* and not the obstreperous author of such an indecent book? I know about all those index cards you carry around in your wallet: fortifying quotations from the great literary snobs about fame giving satisfaction only to mediocre vanities. Well, don't you believe it. There's a lot to be had out of life by a writer in your position, and not at Shloimie's, either. Those buses. To begin with, you should have a car with a driver, Nathan. Thomas Mann had a car with a driver."

"Where'd you hear that?"

"I didn't. I rode in it with him. You should have a girl to answer your mail and run your errands for you. You should have somebody to carry your dirty things down Madison Avenue in a pillowcase—somebody instead of yourself. At least treat yourself to a laundry that picks up sackcloth and delivers."

"They lean on the bell when they pick up—it interrupts my concentration."

"A housekeeper should answer the bell. You should have someone to cook your meals and to shop for your groceries and to deal with the tradesmen at the door. You don't have to push a cart around Gristede's ever again."

"I do if I want to know what a pound of butter costs."

"Why would you want to know that?"

"André, Gristede's is where we poor writers go to lead a real life—don't take Gristede's away from me too. It's how I keep my finger on the pulse of the nation."

"You want to succeed at that, get to know what I know: the price of a pound of flesh. I am being serious. You should have a driver, a housekeeper, a cook, a secretary—"

"And where do I hide in that crowd? Where do I type?"

"Get a bigger place."

"I just got a bigger place. André, that is *more* ridiculousness, not less. I just moved in here. It's quiet, it's plenty big for me, and on East Eighty-first at five hundred a month, it's no slum."

"You should have a duplex at the United Nations Plaza."

"I don't *want* one."

"Nathan, you are no longer the egghead kid I plucked out of the pages of *Esquire*. You have achieved a success as only a handful of writers ever do—so stop acting like those who don't. First you lock yourself away in order to stir up your imagination, now you lock yourself away because you've stirred up theirs. Meanwhile, everybody in the world is dying to meet you. Trudeau was here and he wanted to meet you. Abba Eban was here and mentioned your name to me. Yves Saint Laurent is giving a big party and his office called for your number. But do I dare to give it? And would you even go?"

"Look, I already met Caesara. That should hold me for a while. By the way, tell Mary I received my Dear Juan letter from Havana. She can phone in the news to *Women's Wear Daily*. I'll send them a Xerox by messenger."

"At least Caesara got you out of that cell for one night. I wish I had another lovely lure like her. My dear boy, you live in that apartment, as far as I can tell, thinking about nothing but yourself from one day to the next. And when you even dare to go out into the street, you're worse. Everybody looks at you, everybody sidles up to you, everybody wants either to tie you to a bed or to spit in your eye. Everybody has you pegged for Gilbert Carnovsky, when what anybody with an ounce of brains should know is that you are really you. But if you recall, Nathan dear, being really you was what was driving you crazy only a few short years ago. You told me so yourself. You felt stultified writing 'proper, responsible' novels. You felt stultified living behind your 'drearily virtuous face.' You felt stultified sitting in your chair every night making notes for your files on another Great

159

Book. 'How much more life can I spend preparing for my final exam? I'm too old to be writing term papers.' You felt stultified calling Florida every Sunday like the good son, you felt stultified signing stop-the-war petitions like the good citizen, you felt stultified most of all living with a do-gooder like your wife. The whole country was going haywire and you were still in your chair doing your homework. Well, you have successfully conducted your novelistic experiment and now you are famous all over the haywire country for being highly haywire yourself, and you're even more stultified than before. What is more, you are outraged that everybody doesn't know how proper, responsible, and drearily virtuous you really are, and what a great achievement it is for mankind that such a model of Mature Adult Behavior could have given the reading public a Gilbert Carnovsky. You set out to sabotage your own moralizing nature, you set out to humiliate all your dignified, high-minded gravity, and now that you've done it, and done it with the relish of a real saboteur, now you're humiliated, you idiot, because nobody aside from you seems to see it as a profoundly moral and high-minded act! 'They' misunderstand you. And as for those who do understand you, people who've known you for five and ten and fifteen years, you'll have nothing to do with them, either. As far as I can tell, you don't see a single one of your friends. People call me to ask what's happened to you. Your closest friends think you're out of town. Somebody called me up the other day to ask if it was true that you were in Payne Whitney."

"Oh, am I supposed to be in the bin now too?"

"Nathan, you are the decade's latest celebrity—people are going to say everything. The question I am asking is why you won't at least see old friends."

Simple. Because he couldn't sit complaining to them about becoming the decade's latest celebrity. Because being a poor misunderstood millionaire is not really a topic that intelligent people can discuss for very long. Not even friends. Least of all friends, and especially when they're writers. He didn't want them talking about him talking about his morning with the investment counselor and his night with Caesara O'Shea and how she jilted him for the Revolution. And that was all he could talk about, at least to himself. He was not fit company for anyone he considered a friend. He would get started on all the places where he no longer could show his face without causing a sensation, and soon enough he would make them into enemies. He would get started on the Rollmops King and the gossip columns and the dozen crazy letters a day, and who *could* listen? He would start talking to them about those suits. Six suits. Three thousand dollars' worth of suits to sit at home and write in. When he could write naked, if need be; when he could sit there as he always had, in work shirt and chinos, perfectly content. With three thousand dollars he could have bought one hundred pairs of chinos and four hundred work shirts (he'd worked it out). He could buy sixty pairs of Brooks Brothers suede walking shoes of the kind he'd been wearing since he went off to Chicago. He could buy twelve hundred pairs of Interwoven socks (four hundred blue, four hundred brown, four hundred gray). With three thousand dollars he could have clothed himself for life. But instead there were now fittings with Mr. White twice a week, discussions with Mr. White about padding the shoulders and nipping the waist, and who could possibly listen to Zuckerman carrying on about such stuff? He could hardly listen —

but, alas, alone with himself, he couldn't shut up. Better they should think he was in Payne Whitney. Maybe he ought to be. Because there was also the television—couldn't stop watching. Downtown on Bank Street, all they saw regularly was the news. At seven and again at eleven he and Laura used to sit together in the living room to watch the fires in Vietnam: villages on fire, jungles on fire, Vietnamese on fire. Then they went back to their work on the night shift, she to her draft dodgers, he to his Great Books. During his weeks alone, however, Zuckerman had probably spent more hours by the TV set than in all the years since they had begun to broadcast test patterns back when he was finishing high school. There was little else he could concentrate on, and then there was the strangeness of sitting in your bathrobe on your Oriental rug eating a takeout barbecued chicken and hearing someone suddenly talking about *you*. He couldn't get over it. One night a pretty rock singer whom he'd never seen before told Johnny Carson about her one and "Thank God" only date with Nathan Zuckerman. She brought the house down describing the "gear" Zuckerman advised her to wear to dinner if she wanted "to turn him

163

on." And just the previous Sunday he had watched three therapists sitting in lounge chairs on Channel 5 analyzing his castration complex with the program host. They all agreed that Zuckerman had a lulu. The following morning André's lawyer had gently to tell him that he couldn't sue for slander. "Your nuts, Nathan, are now in the public domain."

They were right in their way—he *was* in the bin.

"The threats, the threats, the *threats*. André," cried Zuckerman, "what about those threats? That is the subject here."

"Delivered as you described them the threats don't seem to me very serious, frankly. But then I am not you, with this sense you have that everything suddenly is beyond your control. If you are feeling the way you sound, then telephone the police and see what they say."

"But you think it's all a joke."

"I wouldn't be surprised."

"And if it isn't? If my mother winds up in the trunk of a car in the Everglades?"

"If this and if that. Do as I say. You want advice, I'm advising you. Phone the police."

"And what can they do? That's the next question."

"I have no idea what they can do when nothing actually has happened to anyone. My concern is defusing the persecution mania, Nathan. That is the job of a literary agent. I should like to restore in you some peace of mind."

"Which calling the police isn't likely to do. Call the police and it's as good as calling the city desk. Call the police and it'll be in Leonard Lyons by tomorrow, if not headlined on page one. PUG THREATENS PORN MOM. The kidnapping of Mrs. Carnovsky—that would really top off the sixties for them. Susskind will have to have three specialists in to think it through with him. 'Who in Our Sick Society Is Responsible?' Sevareid will tell us what it means to the Future of the Free World. Reston will write a column on the Breakdown of Values. If this thing happens, the torment to my mother will be nothing next to what the rest of the country is going to have to put up with."

"Ah, and this is a little more like your old amused self."

"Is it? My old amused self? Wouldn't recognize him. Who is Sleepy Lagoon, while we're at it? What is this in *Variety* about a million dollars for the sequel?"

"Bob Lagoon. I would wait before spending his million."

"But he exists."

"Off and on."

"And Marty Paté? Who is he?"

"Don't know."

"Never heard of a producer on East Sixty-second Street named Marty Paté?"

"As in *'de foie gras'*? Not yet. Why do you ask?"

No, best not to go into that. "What about Gayle Gibraltar?"

André laughed. "Sounds like you're writing a sequel right now. Sounds like some figment of Carnovsky's imagination."

"No, not Carnovsky's. What I ought to do is get a bodyguard. For my mother. Don't you think?"

"Well, if that's what's necessary for your sense of security—"

"Only it's not going to give her much of one, is it? I hate to think of her sitting across from him when he takes off his coat to eat his lunch and she sees the shoulder holster."

"Then why not restrain yourself, Nathan? Why not wait to see if this character phones again? If there is, in fact, no call to make arrangements about extortion money, so much for that. It was somebody's idea of a good time. If there is such a call—"

"Then I notify the police, the F.B.I., and whatever the papers print—"

"Exactly."

"If and when it turns out to be nothing, she'll have been protected just the same."

"And you'll feel that you did the right thing by her."

"Only there it'll be in the papers. Then the bright idea will dawn on some maniac to take a crack at it himself."

"You worry too much about maniacs."

"But they live. The maniacs live better than we do. They flourish. It's their world, André. You should read my mail."

"Nathan, you take everything too seriously, starting with your mail and ending with yourself. Maybe it's starting with yourself and ending with the mail. Maybe that's all the kidnapper is trying to tell you."

"Doing it for my education, is he? You make it sound as though it might even be you."

"I'd like to say that it was. I wish I were clever enough to have thought of it."

"I wish you were too. I wish somebody were, other than whoever it is."

"Or isn't."

As soon as he hung up, Zuckerman began searching for the card presented him by Caesara O'Shea's chauffeur. He should call to ask them to recommend an armed guard in Miami. He should fly to Miami himself. He should telephone the Miami field office of the F.B.I. He should stop eating in delicatessens. He should furnish his apartment. He should unpack his books. He should take his money out of his shoe and give it to Wallace to invest. He should forget about Caesara and get a new girl. There were hundreds of not-so-crazy Julias out there just waiting to take him to Switzerland and show him the chocolate factories. He should stop buying chickens from takeout counters. He should meet U Thant. He should stop taking seriously all the talk-show de Tocquevilles. He should stop taking seriously the cranks on the phone. He should stop taking his mail seriously. He should stop taking himself seriously. He should stop taking buses. And he should call André back and tell him for God's sake not to tell Mary anything about the kidnapper—otherwise it would end up in "Suzy Says"!

But instead he sat back down at his desk and for another hour recorded in his composition book everything the kidnapper had said. In spite of his worries, he was smiling to himself as he saw on paper what he'd heard the night before on the phone. He was reminded of a story about Flaubert coming out of his study one day and seeing a cousin of his, a young married woman, tending to her children, and Flaubert saying, ruefully, *"Ils sont dans le vrai."* A working title, Zuckerman thought, and recorded in the white window of the composition book cover the words *Dans le Vrai.* These composition books Zuckerman used for his notes were bound in the stiff covers of marbled black-and-white design that generations of Americans envision still in bad dreams about lessons unlearned. On the inside of the front cover, facing the blue ruled lines of the first page, was the chart where the student is to enter his class program, period by period, for the school week. Here Zuckerman composed his subtitle, printing in block letters across the rows of rectangles provided for the subject, room, and instructor: "Or, How I Made a Fiasco of Fame and Fortune in My Spare Time."

"'Tzena, Tzena,' 1950."

Zuckerman was waiting for the light to change on the corner across from Campbell's. The title had been announced from just behind him. Unknown to himself, he had been whistling, and not only out on the street but through much of the morning. That same little song, again and again.

"Adapted from an Israeli popular tune, English lyrics by Mitchell Parish, Decca record by Gordon Jenkins and the Weavers."

There to inform him was Alvin Pepler. The day was fresh and bright, but Pepler was still in black raincoat and hat. Dark glasses, however, to top things off this morning. Had somebody poked him in the eye since last night, some shorter-fused celebrity than Zuckerman? Or were the dark glasses to make him look like a celebrity to himself? Or was the new pitch that he was, also, unfortunately, blind? SIGHTLESS QUIZ CONTESTANT. PLEASE GIVE.

"Good morning," said Zuckerman, backing away.

170

"Up early for the great event?"

One-liner, delivered with comic grin. Zuckerman chose not to reply.

"Imagine, you go out for a coffee break and run smack into Prince Seratelli lying in state."

You go for a coffee break on Sixty-second Street and run into Seratelli on Eighty-first?

"That's why I envy you New Yorkers," said Pepler. "You get into an elevator—this actually happened to me, my first day over here—and there, sharp as a tack, Victor Borge! You run out for the late paper, and who jumps from a taxi right at your feet? At midnight? Twiggy! You walk out of the bathroom in a little delicatessen, and sitting there eating is you! Victor Borge, Twiggy, and you—just in my first forty-eight hours. The cop on the horse told me rumor has it that Sonny Liston is supposed to show." He pointed to the police and the onlookers gathered at the main entrance to the funeral home. Also on hand was a TV camera and crew. "But so far," said Pepler, "you haven't missed a thing."

Not a word about Zuckerman's disappearance outside Baskin-Robbins the previous evening. Or about the phone calls.

Zuckerman assumed Pepler had followed him. Dark glasses for dark intrigue. The possibility had crossed his mind before he'd even left the house: Pepler in a doorway along the street, hiding and ready to pounce. But he couldn't sit there waiting for the phone to ring just because the kidnapper had told him to. That *was* nuts. Especially if the kidnapper was this crackpot.

"What else do you know from 1950?"

"Pardon?"

"What other songs," Pepler asked him, "from 1950? Can you name me the Top Fifteen?"

Followed or not, Zuckerman had to smile. "You got me there. From 1950 I couldn't name the Top Ten."

"Want to hear which they were? All fifteen?"

"I have to be going."

"To begin with, that's the year there are three with 'cake' in the title. 'Candy and Cake.' 'If I Knew You Were Comin' I'd 'Ave Baked a Cake.' And 'Sunshine Cake.' Then, alphabetically"—for this he planted both feet firmly on the pavement—"'Autumn Leaves,' 'A Bushel and a Peck,' 'C'est Si Bon,' 'It's a Lovely Day Today,' 'Music, Music, Music,'

'My Heart Cries for You,' 'Rag Mop,' 'Sam's Song,' 'The Thing,' 'Tzena, Tzena'—which I began with—'Wilhelmina,' and 'You, Wonderful You.' Fifteen. And Hewlett Lincoln couldn't have named you five. Without the answers in his pocket, he couldn't have named *one*. No, with the All-Time American Hit Parade, it was Alvin Pepler who was Mr. Unstoppable. Until they stopped me to get the goy on."

"I'd forgotten 'Rag Mop,'" said Zuckerman.

Pepler laughed his hearty appreciative laugh. God, he certainly seemed harmless enough. Dark glasses? A tourist indulgence. Going native. "Whistle something else," Pepler said. "Anything. As far back in time as you want."

"I really have to be off."

"Please, Nathan. Just to test me out. To prove to you I'm on the level. That I am Pepler in the flesh!"

Well, the war was on, the sirens had sounded, and his father, the street's chief air-raid warden, was out of the house in the prescribed sixty seconds. Henry, Nathan, and their mother sat at the rickety bridge table in the basement, playing casino by candlelight. Only a drill, not the real thing, never the real thing in America, but of course, if you were a ten-year-old American you never knew. They could miss Newark Airport and hit the Zuckerman house. But soon the All Clear sounded and Dr. Zuckerman came whistling down the cellar stairs in his warden hat, playfully shining his flashlight into the boys' eyes. No plane had been sighted, no bombs had been dropped, the decrepit Sonnenfelds down the street had pulled their blackout shades on their own, and neither of his sons had as yet written a book or touched a girl, let alone divorced one. So why shouldn't he be whistling? He turned on the lights and kissed them each in turn. "Deal me in," he said.

The song his father whistled descending their cellar stairs Nathan whistled now for Pepler. Instead of running.

Three notes was all he had to deliver. "'I'll Be Seeing You,' 1943. Twenty-four appearances on the Hit Parade," said Pepler, "ten in the Number One spot. Records by Frank Sinatra and by Hildegarde. The Top Fifteen, 1943—ready, Nathan?"

Oh, was he ready. *Dans le vrai,* and it's about time too. André was right to give it to him: you lock yourself away to stir up your

174

imagination, then you lock yourself away because you've stirred up theirs. What kind of novels is that going to get you? If the high life with Caesara hadn't worked out, then what about the low? Where is your curiosity? Where is your old amused self? Against whom have you committed what punishable offense that you should go skulking around like a fugitive from justice? You are not in the virtue racket! Never were! Great mistake ever to think so! That is what you have escaped—into the stupendous *vrai!* "Shoot, Alvin." Reckless locution, but Zuckerman didn't care. Reckless deliberately. Enough taking cover from his own eruption. Receive what has been given! Accept what you inspire! Welcome the genies released by that book! That goes for the money, that goes for the fame, and that goes for this Angel of Manic Delights!

Who was off and running anyway:

"'Comin' in on a Wing and a Prayer.' 'I Couldn't Sleep a Wink Last Night.' 'I'll Be Seeing You.' 'It's Love, Love, Love.' 'I've Heard That Song Before.' 'A Lovely Way to Spend an Evening.' 'Mairzy Doats.' 'Oh, What a Beautiful Mornin',' by the way, not 'Morning,' as most people think—Hewlett Lincoln being Number One. Though nobody of course called him on it. Not on that show. 'People Will Say We're in Love.' 'Pistol Packin' Mama.' 'Sunday, Monday or Always.' 'They're Either Too Young or Too Old.' 'Tico Tico.' 'You Keep Coming Back Like a Song.' 'You'll Never Know.' Fifteen." He relaxed, sagged a little, in fact, remembering what Hewlett had gotten away with on that show.

"How do you do it, Alvin?"

Pepler removed his dark glasses, and rolling his dark eyes (which no one had yet blackened), made a joke. "'It's Magic,'" he confessed.

Zuckerman obliged. "Doris Day. Nineteen—forty-six."

"Close," cried Pepler gaily, "close, but forty-eight is the correct answer. Awfully sorry, Nathan. Better luck next time. Words by Sammy Cahn, music by Jule Styne. Introduced in the movie *Romance on the High Seas*. Warner Brothers. With Jack Carson, and of course the Divine Dodo, Miss Doris Day."

He had Zuckerman laughing away now. "Alvin, you're amazing."

To which Pepler rapidly replied, "'You're Sensational.' 'You're Devastating.' 'You're

My Everything.' 'You're Nobody Till Some-
body Loves You.' 'You're Breaking My Heart.'
'You're Getting to Be a Habit with Me.'
'You're—'"

"This, this is quite a show. Oh, this is
heaven, really." He couldn't stop laughing.
Not that Pepler seemed to mind.

"'—a Grand Old Flag.' 'You're a Million
Miles from Nowhere (When You're One Little
Mile from Home).' 'You're My Thrill.' Do I
stop?" Agleam with perspiration, about as
happy as any adrenalin addict could ever be,
he asked, "Do I stop, kid, or do you want
more?"

"No," groaned Zuckerman, "no more," but
oh, was it lovely to be having a good time.
And out-of-doors! In public! Sprung! Free!
Released from his captivity by Pepler! "Take
it easy on me. Please, please," Zuckerman
whispered, "there's a funeral across the street."

"Street," announced Pepler. "'The Streets
of New York.' Across. 'Across the Alley from
the Alamo.' Funeral. Let me think that
through. Please. 'Please Don't Talk About Me
When I'm Gone.' More. 'The More I See You.'
No. 'No Other Love.' Now funeral. No, I stake
my reputation on it. There is no song in the

177

history of American popular songs with the word 'funeral' in it. For obvious reasons."

Priceless. The *vrai*. You can't beat it. Even richer in pointless detail than the great James Joyce.

"Correction," said Pepler. "'The More I See *of* You.' From the motion picture *Diamond Horseshoe*. Twentieth Century-Fox. 1945. Sung by Dick Haymes."

No stopping him now. But why should anyone want to? No, you don't run away from phenomena like Alvin Pepler, not if you're a novelist with any brains you don't. Think how far Hemingway went to look for a lion. Whereas Zuckerman had just stepped out the door. Yes, sir, box up the books! Out of the study and into the streets! At one with the decade at last! Oh, what a novel this guy would make! All that flies, sticks. He's glue, mental flypaper, can't forget a thing. All the interfering static, he collects. What a *novelist* this guy would make! Already is one! Paté, Gibraltar, Perlmutter, Moshe Dayan—that is the novel of which he is the hero! From the daily papers and the dregs of memory, that is the novel that he conjures up! Can't say it lacks conviction, whatever may be missing in the way of finesse. Look at him go!

178

"'You'll Never Know,' Decca, 1943. 'Little White Lies,' Decca, 1948." Dick Haymes's two best-selling records, according to Pepler. Whom Zuckerman saw no reason not to believe.

"Perry Como," Zuckerman asked. "*His* best-sellers."

"'Temptation.' 'A Hubba Hubba Hubba.' 'Till the End of Time.' All RCA Victor, 1945. 1946, 'Prisoner of Love.' 1947, 'When You Were Sweet Sixteen.' 1949—"

Zuckerman had forgotten the kidnapper completely. For the moment he forgot everything, all his cares and woes. They were imaginary anyway, no?

Pepler was on to Nat "King" Cole—"'Darling, Je Vous Aime Beaucoup,' 1955; 'Ramblin' Rose,' 1962"—when Zuckerman discovered the microphone an inch from his mouth. Then the portable camera aimed from atop somebody's shoulder.

"Mr. Zuckerman, you're here to pay your respects this morning to Prince Seratelli—"

"I am?"

The dark-haired reporter, a handsome and powerful-looking fellow, Zuckerman now recognized from one of the local news shows. "Is it," asked the reporter, "as a friend of the deceased or of the family?"

The comedy was too much. Oh, what a morning. "Oh, What a Beautiful Mornin'!" *Oklahoma!* Rodgers and Hammerstein. Even he knew that one.

Laughing, waving a hand in the air to call them off, Zuckerman said, "No, no, just passing by." He gestured toward Pepler. "With a friend."

All too distinctly he heard the friend clear his throat. The dark glasses were off, the chest had expanded, and he looked ready to remind the world of all it had caused him to suffer. Zuckerman saw the crowd at Campbell's turning in their direction.

A voice from across the way. *"Who?"*

"Koufax! Koufax!"

"Mistake, mistake." Zuckerman was a little on the fervent side now, but the aggressive reporter seemed at last to have realized his error himself and signaled to the cameraman to stop.

"Sorry, sir," he said to Zuckerman.

"That ain't Koufax, idiot."

"Who is it?"

"Nobody."

"Awfully sorry," said the reporter, apologetically smiling to Pepler now as the crew moved swiftly back to where the real action was getting underway. A limousine had arrived across the street. Everyone by the doorway tried to see if it was Sonny Liston inside.

"That," said Pepler, pointing after the TV reporter, "was J. K. Cranford. The All-American from Rutgers."

A mounted policeman had by now approached the two of them, and was leaning down from his horse to get a good look. "Hey, Mac," he said to Zuckerman, "who are you?"

"Nobody to worry about." Zuckerman patted the breast pocket of his corduroy jacket to show that he wasn't packing a gat.

The cop was willing to be amused; not nearly so much as Zuckerman's sidekick. "I mean, who are you famous?" he asked. "You were just on the TV, right?"

"No, no," explained Zuckerman. "They had the wrong guy."

"You weren't on Dinah Shore last week?"

"Not me, officer. I was home in bed."

Pepler just couldn't let this big tough cop up on a horse make any more of a fool of himself. "You don't know who this guy is? This is Nathan Zuckerman!"

The cop looked down with bemused boredom at the man in the dark glasses and the black rain gear.

"The *writer*," Pepler informed him.

"Oh, yeah?" said the cop. "What'd he write?"

"You serious? What did Nathan Zuckerman write?" With such triumph did Pepler announce the title of Zuckerman's fourth book that the powerful sleek horse, trained though it was for civil disorder, reared sharply back and had to be reined in.

"Never heard of it," the cop replied and, swinging around, crossed handsomely back to Campbell's with the light.

Pepler, with disdain: "It's the horses they must mean are New York's finest."

Together they looked across to where All-American J. K. Cranford was interviewing a little man who had just popped out of a taxi. Manuel Somebody, Pepler said. The jockey. Pepler was surprised that he had arrived without his glamorous wife, the dancer.

After the jockey, a silver-haired gentleman, staidly dressed in a dark suit and vest. To Cranford's questions, he mournfully shook his head. Wasn't talking. "Who's he?" Zuckerman asked.

A Mob lawyer, he was told, recently released from a federal penitentiary. He looked to Zuckerman, what with the deep tan, to have recently been released from the Bahamas.

For the next few minutes Pepler identified the mourners as each was accosted by Cranford and his crew.

"You are something, Alvin."

"You think so—from *this*? You should have seen me on 'Smart Money.' This is just a *sample*. Hewlett *needed* the fix, the fake. When Schachtman came around on Sundays to deliver the answers, half the time I had to correct him, where they had something wrong. If I see a face, that's it. I know the face of anybody in the world who has ever been in the papers, whether it's a cardinal who ran for Pope or some stewardess from Belgium who went down in a crash. With my memory, it's indelible, it's there forever. I can't forget it even if I wanted to. You should have seen me at my height, Nathan, what I was like for those three weeks. I lived from Thursday to Thursday. 'He's terrifying, he knows everything.' That's how they would introduce me on the show. To them it was just more crapola to feed the idiot audience. The tragedy is that it happened to be true. And what I didn't know, I could learn. You only had to show it

183

to me, you just had to push the right button and out came a flood of information. I could tell you, for example, everything in history that ever happened with the number 98 in it. I still can. Everybody knows 1066, but do they know 1098? Everybody knows 1492, but do they know 1498? Savonarola burned at the stake in Florence, first German pawnshop established at Nuremberg, Vasco da Gama discovers sea route to India. But why go on? What good did it do me in the end? 1598: Shakespeare writes *Much Ado about Nothing,* Korean Admiral Visunsin invents iron-clad warships. 1698: Paper manufacturing begins in North America, Leopold of Anhalt-Dessau introduces goose-stepping and iron ramrods in the Prussian army. 1798: Casanova dies, Battle of Pyramids makes Napoleon master of Egypt. I could go on all day. All night. But what will it get me? What good is all the learning if it only goes to waste? At last people in New Jersey were beginning to have a respect for knowledge, for history, for the real facts of life instead of their own stupid, narrow, prejudiced opinions. Because of me! And now, now? You know where I should be now, by all rights? Across the street. I should be J. K. Cranford!"

So hungrily did he look to Zuckerman for confirmation that there was nothing to say in reply but "I don't see why not."

"You *don't?*"

And to that impassioned plea? "Why not?" replied Zuckerman.

"Oh, Jesus, would you do me a favor, Nathan? Would you spend one minute reading something I wrote? Would you give me your candid opinion? It would mean the world to me. Not my book, something else. Something new."

"What?"

"Well, literary criticism, actually."

Gently. "You didn't tell me you were a literary critic too."

Another Zuckerman one-liner, which Pepler accorded its due. Dared even to counter with one of his own. "I thought you already knew. I thought that's why last night you took it on the lam." But then added, when Zuckerman remained sternly silent, "I'm only kidding you back, Nathan. I realized when I came out, you had business, your meeting, you had to run. So you know me: I ate your ice cream too. And paid for it all night. No, don't worry, I'm no critic. I have my likes and dislikes, I have my ulcer, but I'm no critic, not in the official sense. However, I did hear yesterday about the big shake-up at the *Times*. This is ancient history to you, but I only found out late last night."

"What shake-up?"

"The drama critic is going to get the boot, and probably the book reviewer too. It's been a long time coming."

"Yes?"

"You didn't know?"

"No."

"*Really?* Well, I heard from Mr. Perlmutter. He's in with Sulzberger, the owner. He knows the whole family. They belong to the same congregation."

Perlmutter? Mythical gentlemanly father of the mythical producer Paté? Knows Sulzberger too? This novel is some novel.

"So you're going to try for the job," said Zuckerman.

Pepler colored. "No, no, not at all. It just got me thinking. To see if I could do it. 'I'll study and get ready, and maybe the chance will come.' Strange, even to me, that I haven't become a cynic after all I've been through, that I am still this sucker for the Land of Opportunity. But how could I feel otherwise? I know this country inside out. I served this country in two wars. It isn't just popular songs—it's everything. It's sports, it's old-time radio, it's slang, proverbs, commercials, famous ships, the Constitution, great battles, longitudes and latitudes—you name it, and if it's Americana, I know it cold. And *without* the answers in my pocket. With them in my *head*. I believe in this country. I believe in it because for one thing it is a country where a man can fight back from the most ignominious defeat, if only he perseveres. If only he doesn't lose faith in himself. Look at history. Look at Nixon. Isn't that something, that survival story? I have fifteen pages on that fake in my book. Likewise the great shit slinger, Johnson. Now, where would Lyndon Johnson have been without Lee Harvey Oswald? Peddling real estate in the Senate cloakroom."

Oswald? Had Alvin Pepler just mentioned Lee Harvey Oswald? On the phone last night, hadn't his caller referred in passing to Ruby, "Jack Idiot Ruby," as America's new patron saint? And alluded to Sirhan Sirhan? *We had a great leader in Robert Kennedy and that crazy Arab bastard shot him.* It was all in Zuckerman's notes.

Time to go.

But what danger was there? Weren't there

cops everywhere? But weren't they also there in Dallas, for all the good that did the President?

Oh, and was his position in America now commensurate with the Presidency, the author of *Carnovsky?*

"—my book review."

"Yes?" He'd lost the thread. His heartbeat had quickened too.

"I only began writing at midnight last night."

After your last phone call, thought Zuckerman. Yes, yes, the man before me is my mother's kidnapper. Who else?

"I haven't had time to get to the novel itself. These are simply first impressions. If they sound too cerebral, well, I realize that. It's just that I'm bending over backward while I'm writing not to say in print what of course is no great secret, at least to me. That in many ways that book is the story of my life no less than yours."

So the review was of Zuckerman's book, of all books. Time to go, all right. Forget Oswald and Ruby. When the lion comes up to Hemingway with his review of "The Short Happy Life of Francis Macomber," time to leave the jungle for home.

"I don't mean Newark alone. It goes without saying how much that meant personally to me. I mean...the hang-ups. The psychological ones," he said, flushing, "of a nice Jewish boy. I guess everybody has identified with that book in his own way. That's what has made it such a smash. What I mean is that if I ever had the talent to write a novel, well, *Carnovsky* would have been it."

Zuckerman looked at his watch. "Alvin, I've got to be off."

"But my review."

"Send it, why don't you." Out of the streets and into the study. Time to unbox the books.

"But here, it's here." Pepler extracted the small spiral notebook from an inside breast pocket. Instantly he found the page and handed it to Zuckerman to read.

There was a mailbox at Zuckerman's back. Pepler had pinned him up against the mailbox, just as he had the evening before. The evening before! *The man is mad. And fixed on me. Who is he behind those dark glasses? Me! He thinks he's me!*

Suppressing the impulse to drop the notebook into the mailbox and just walk off, a free celebrity, he looked down and he read. Been reading all his life. Really, what danger was there?

"The Marcel Proust of New Jersey" was the title of Pepler's review.

"All I have so far is my opening paragraph," he explained. "But if in your opinion I am off on the right foot, then tonight I'll finish it up at Paté's. Friday Perlmutter can show it to Sulzberger."

"I see."

Pepler saw too—Zuckerman's incredulity. And rushed to reassure him. "Bigger jerks than me review books, Nathan."

Well, on that he was not going to get an argument. Pepler's one-liner made Zuckerman laugh aloud. And Zuckerman was no enemy of laughs, as the fans would attest. So, up against the mailbox, he plunged in. One more page wouldn't kill him.

The handwriting was minute, fussy, meticulous, anything but seething. Nor was the style the man, either.

Fiction is not autobiography, yet all fiction, I am convinced, is in some sense rooted in autobiography, though the connection to actual events may be tenuous indeed, even nonexistent. We are, after all, the total of our experiences, and experience includes not only what we in fact do but what we privately imagine. An author cannot write about what he does not know and the reader must grant him his material, yet there are dangers in writing so closely on the heels of one's own immediate experience: a lack of toughness, perhaps; a tendency to indulgence; an urge to justify the author's ways to men. Distance, on the other hand, either blurs experience or heightens it. For most of us it is mercifully blurred; but for writers, if they can be restrained from spilling the beans before they are digested, it is heightened.

Before Zuckerman could even speak—not that he was in any hurry to—Pepler was explaining his methodology. "I discuss the autobiographical problem before I get to the contents of the book. That I'll do tonight. It's all worked out in my mind. What I am trying is to begin with my literary theory, to create a mini-version of my own of *What Is Art?* by Leo Tolstoy, first published in English translation in 1898. What's wrong?" he said, when Zuckerman handed the notebook back to him.

"Nothing. It's fine. Good beginning."

"You don't believe that." He opened the

notebook and looked at his own handwriting, so neat, so readable, so determinedly everything that Teacher could least expect from the big ungainly boy at the back of the room. "What's wrong with it? You've got to tell me. I don't want Sulzberger to read it if it stinks. I want the truth. I have been fighting and suffering for the truth all my life. Please, no sweet talk and no crapola, either. What's wrong? So I can learn, so I can improve myself and recover my rightful place!"

No, he hadn't plagiarized it. Not that it made any difference, but evidently he had cooked up this porridge all by himself, one eye on *The New York Times,* the other on Leo Tolstoy. At midnight, after the last villainous haw, haw, haw. *I will do everything in my power to avoid violence, but if I feel threatened I am going to have to act like a threatened man.* That was what was down in *Zuckerman's* notebook.

"As I say, it's not bad, not at all."

"It is! You know it is! Only tell me *why.* How will I learn if you don't tell me why!"

"Well," said Zuckerman, relenting, "I suppose I wouldn't call the writing laconic, Alvin."

"You wouldn't?"

He shook his head.

"Is that bad?"

Zuckerman tried to sound thoughtful. "No, of course it's not 'bad'..."

"But it's not good. Okay. All right. What about my ideas, what I want to communicate. The writing I can polish in the next draft, when I have the time. The writing I can get Miss Diamond to fix, if you say that's what it needs. But surely the ideas, the ideas themselves..."

"The ideas," said Zuckerman somberly, as the notebook was handed to him again. Across the street an elderly woman was being interviewed by J. K. Cranford instead of by Alvin Pepler. Gaunt, handsome, supported by a cane. Seratelli's widow? Seratelli's mother? Would that I were that old lady, thought Zuckerman. Anything but to have to discuss these "ideas."

Fiction, Zuckerman silently read, *is not autobiography, yet all fiction, I am convinced, is in some sense rooted in autobiography, though the connection to actual events...*

"Forget the writing for now," Pepler told him. "This time just read it through for the thoughts."

Zuckerman looked blindly at the page.

193

Heard the lion saying to Hemingway, "Just read it through for the thoughts."

"I read it for both already." He put a hand on Pepler's chest and gently pushed him back. Not the best idea, he knew, but what else could he do? This enabled him to step away from the mailbox. He handed back the notebook yet again. Pepler looked as though he'd been pole-axed.

"And?"

"And what?" said Zuckerman.

"The truth! This is my *life* we're talking about, my chance at a second chance. I must have the truth!"

"Well, the truth is"—but seeing the perspiration coursing down Pepler's face, he thought better of it, and concluded—"it's probably fine for the papers."

"But? There's a big but in your voice, Nathan. But *what?*"

Zuckerman counted the cops with pistols outside Frank Campbell's. On foot, four. On horseback, two. "Well, I don't think you have to go into the desert and stand on a pillar to come up with these 'thoughts.' In my opinion. Since you ask for it."

"Whooff." Feverishly he began tapping the notebook against his open palm. "You shoot
194

from the hip all right. Whew. That book of yours doesn't come from nowhere, that's for sure. The satire, I mean. Wow."

"Alvin, listen to me. Sulzberger could be crazy about it. I'm sure he and I have different criteria entirely. This shouldn't discourage you from letting Perlmutter try him."

"Nah," he said despondently. "When it comes to writing, it's you who's the authority." As though plunging a knife into his chest, he shoved the notebook back in his pocket.

"Not everybody would agree there."

"Nah, nah, don't pull the little-me stuff. Don't give me the humble crap. We know who's tops in his field and who isn't." Whereupon he drew the notebook out again and began fiercely slapping at it with his free hand. "What about when I say the writer should be restrained from spilling the beans before they are digested? What about *that?*"

Zuckerman the satirist remained silent.

"That stinks too?" asked Pepler. "Don't condescend to me, *tell* me!"

"Of course it doesn't 'stink.'"

"*But?*"

"But it's straining, isn't it, for an effect?" As serious and uncondescending a man of let-

195

ters as there could ever be, Zuckerman said, "I wonder if it's worth the effort."

"There's where you're wrong. It was no strain at all. It just came to me. In those words. It's the only line here that *isn't* erased, not one word."

"Then maybe that's the problem."

"I see." Pepler nodded vigorously because of what he saw. "For me, if it comes easy it's no good, and if it comes hard it's also no good."

"I'm only talking about this line."

"I see-ee-ee-eee," he said, ominously. "But that's definitely the worst, the bottom, the limit, this line about spilling the beans."

"Sulzberger could see it differently."

"Fuck Sulzberger! I'm not asking Sulzberger! I'm asking you! And what you have told me is the following. One, the writing stinks. Two, the thoughts stink. Three, my best line stinks worst of all. What you have told me is that ordinary mortals like me shouldn't even dare to write about your book to begin with. Isn't that what it adds up to, *on the basis of one paragraph of a first draft?*"

"Why, no."

"Why, no." Pepler was mimicking him. He had removed his dark glasses to make a prissy face to show to Zuckerman. "Why, no."

"Don't turn nasty, Alvin. You wanted the truth, after all."

"After all. After all."

"Look," said Zuckerman, "you want the *whole* truth?"

"Yes!" Eyes big, eyes bulging, eyes asizzle in a glowing red face. "Yes! But the truth *unbiased,* that's what I want! Unbiased by the fact that you only wrote that book because you could! Because of having every break in life there is! While the ones who didn't obviously couldn't! Unbiased by the fact that those hang-ups you wrote about happen to be mine, and that you knew it—that you stole it!"

"I did what? Stole what?"

"From what my Aunt Lottie told your cousin Essie that she told to your mother that she told to you. About me. About my past."

Oh, was it time to go!

The light was red. Would it never be green again when he needed it? With no further criticism to make or instruction to give, Zuckerman turned to leave.

"Newark!" Pepler, behind him, delivered the word straight to the eardrum. "What do you know about Newark, Mama's Boy! I read that fucking book! To you it's Sunday chop

197

suey downtown at the Chink's! To you it's being Leni-Lenape Indians at school in the play! To you it's Uncle Max in his undershirt, watering the radishes at night! And Nick Etten at first for the Bears! Nick Etten! Moron! *Moron!* Newark is a nigger with a knife! Newark is a whore with the syph! Newark is junkies shitting in your hallway and everything burned to the ground! Newark is dago vigilantes hunting jigs with tire irons! Newark is bankruptcy! Newark is ashes! Newark is rubble and filth! Own a car in Newark and then you'll find out what Newark's all about! Then you can write *ten* books about Newark! They slit your throat for your radial tires! They cut off both balls for a Bulova watch! And your dick for the fun of it, if it's white!"

The light went green. Zuckerman made for the mounted policeman. "You! Whining about Mama back in Newark and how she wouldn't wipe your ass for you three times a day! Newark is finished, idiot! Newark is barbarian hordes and the Fall of Rome! But what the hell would you know up on the hoity-toity East Side of Manhattan? You fuck up Newark and you steal my life—"

Past the prancing horse, the gaping crowd, past J. K. Cranford and his camera crew ("Hi, there, Nathan"), past the uniformed porter, and into the funeral parlor.

The large foyer looked like a Broadway theater at opening-night intermission: backers and burghers in their finest, and conversation bubbling, as though the first act had been a million laughs and the show on its way to being a hit.

He made for an empty corner, and one of the young funeral directors immediately started toward him through the crowd. Zuckerman had seen the fellow around, usually outside in the afternoon, talking through the cab window of a truck with the casket deliveryman. One evening he'd caught sight of him, dragging on a cigarette and with his tie undone, holding open the side door for the arrival of a corpse. When the lead stretcherbearer stumbled on the doorsill, the body stirred slightly in its sack and Zuckerman had thought of his father.

For the lying-in-state of Prince Seratelli, the young funeral director wore a carnation and a morning coat. Strong jaw, athletic build, the voice a countertenor's. "Mr. Zuckerman?"

"Yes?"

"Anything I can do for you, sir?"

"No, no, thank you. Just paying my respects."

He nodded. Whether he bought it was another matter. Zuckerman unshaven didn't look that respectful.

"If you prefer, sir, when you're ready to leave, you can depart through the rear."

"No, no. Only collecting myself. I'll be fine."

Eyeing the door, Zuckerman waited it out with the mobsters and the ex-cons and the other celebrities. You would think he actually *was* being stalked by an Oswald. That he *was* a Kennedy, or a Martin Luther King. But wasn't he just that to Pepler? And what was Oswald, before he pulled the trigger and made it big in the papers? And not on the book page, either. Any less affronted, or benighted, or aggrieved? Any less batty or more impressive? Motivated any more "meaningfully"? No! Bang bang, you're dead. There was all the meaning the act was ever meant to have. You're you, I'm me, and for that and that alone you die. Even the professional killers with whom he now was rubbing elbows were less to be feared. Not that it was necessarily in his interest to hang around them much longer, either. Unshaven, in a worn corduroy suit and a turtleneck sweater and battered suede shoes, he could easily be taken for a nosy newsman rather than someone still studying for his final exam. Especially as he was busily taking notes on the back of a Frank E. Campbell brochure, while waiting for the coast to clear. Another writer with his urgent "thoughts."

Remembrance of Hits Past. My pickle his madeleine. Why isn't P. Proust of the Pops instead of a file cabinet? The uneventfulness of writing, he couldn't put up with it. Who can? Maniacal memory without maniacal desire for comprehension. Drowning without detachment. Memory coheres around nothing (except Dostoevskian despair over fame). With him no things past. All now. P. memory of what hasn't happened to him, Proust of all that has. Knowledge of people out of "People" page in *Time*. Another contending personality for ringside at Elaine's. But: the bullying ego, the personal audacity, the natural coarseness, the taste for exhausting encounters—what gifts! Mix with talent the unstoppable energy, the flypaper brain...but he knows that too. It's the talentlessness that's driving him nuts. The brute strength, the crazy tenacity, the desperate hunger—

201

producers figured right he'd scare the country to death. The Jew You Can't Permit in
the Parlor. How Johnny Carson America
now thinks of me. This Peplerian barrage is
what? Zeitgeist overspill? Newark polter-
geist? Tribal retribution? Secret sharer? P.
as my pop self? Not far from how P. sees it.
He who's made fantasy of others now fantasy
of others. Book: *The Vrai's Revenge*—the
forms their fascination takes, the counter-
spell cast over me.

When he spotted the young funeral director, he signaled by raising one hand. Not too
high, however.

He would take the rear exit, no matter how
dark or dank the subterranean corridors he
had to escape through.

But it was only a bright carpeted hallway
into which he was led, with cubicle doors on
both sides. No ghoul emerged to take his measurements. It could have been an office of the
I.R.S.

His young guide pointed to the cubicle that
was his. "Could you wait, sir, just one second?
Something from my desk." He returned carrying a copy of *Carnovsky*. "If you would... 'For
John P. Driscoll'... Oh, that's awfully kind."

* * *

On Fifth he found a taxi. "Bank Street. Step on it." The driver, an elderly black man, was amused by the gangster locution and, for the fun of it seemingly, drove him to the Village in record time. Time enough, however, for Zuckerman to gauge what he'd be up against with Laura. *I don't want to be beaten over the head with how boring I was for three years.* You weren't boring for three years. *I don't please you anymore, Nathan. It's as simple as that.* Are we talking about sex? Let's then. *There's nothing to say about it. I can do it and you can do it. I'm sure there are people both of us could call in to verify that. The rest I refuse to hear. Your present state has made you forget just how much I bored you. My affectless manner, as it is called, bored you. The way I tell a story bored you. My conversation and my ideas bored you. My work bored you. My friends bored you. My taste in clothes bored you. The way I make love bored you. Not making love to me bored you more.* The way you make love did not bore me. Far from it. *But then it did. Something did, Nathan. You have a way of making things like that*

203

very clear. When you're dissatisfied, your manner is by no means affectless, to use the word. It was the wrong word. I'm sorry about that word. *Don't be. It's what you meant. Nathan, stop pretending. You were bored to tears and you need a new life.* I was wrong. I need you. I thrived on you. I love you. *Oh, please don't try to break me down by saying reckless things. I've had a rough time too. I'd like to think that the hardest part is over. It has to be. I couldn't take those first few weeks again.* Well, I couldn't take those, I can't take these, and the ones looming ahead I don't intend to take. *You'll have to. I beg of you, don't try to kiss me, don't try to hold me, don't ever again tell me you love me. If you try to break me down that way I'll have to cut you out of my life completely.* But that's the answer, isn't it? Maybe what you call "broken down," Laura— *Once is enough, thank you. Once is enough to be told you won't do. You may finally be suffering from the fallout of leaving, but I haven't changed. I am still the same person who won't do. I am relentlessly reasonable and emotionally unflappable, if not seriously repressed. I still have my executive mind and my deadpan delivery and my do-good Christianity, all of which won't do. I am still in the "virtue*
204

racket." That was the wrong word too. I was cursing myself more than you. *It amounts to the same thing, doesn't it? It amounts to why I became so "boring."* And that was the wrong word. Laura, I have made a terrible mistake. The words were brutally wrong. *No, they were brutally right, and you know it. After the clinging, quivering wives, I was just perfect. No tears, no fits, no euphoria, no crises in restaurants or at parties. You could get your work done with me. You could concentrate and live within yourself all you wanted. I didn't even care about having children. I had work of my own to accomplish. I never needed to be entertained, and I didn't have to entertain you, beyond a few minutes in the morning, playing wake-up games in bed. Which I loved. I loved being Lorelei, Nathan. I loved it all, and even longer than you did. But that's behind us. Now you need another dramatic personality.* I need no such thing. I need you. *Let me finish. You bawl me out for being an affectless goody-good Pollyanna WASP, and never saying all that's on my mind. Let me, and then it'll never have to be said again. You want to be renewed, it's what your work requires now. Whatever is finished for you there has finished it for you with someone like me. You don't want our life any-*

more. You think you do today because nothing has come along to take its place, except all this flap about your book. But when something does, you'll see that I'm right to refuse to let you come back. That you were perfectly right to go: having written a book like that, you had to go. That's what writing it was all about.

And how was he going to argue with that? Everything she would say sounded so honest and persuasive, and everything he would say sounded so disingenuous and feeble. He could only hope that she wouldn't be able to make the case against him as well as he himself could. But knowing her, there wasn't much chance of that. Oh, his brave, lucid, serious, good-hearted Lorelei! But he had thrown her away. By writing a book ostensibly about someone else attempting to break free from his accustomed constraints.

At Bank Street he tipped the cabbie five dollars for valor on the West Side Highway. He could as easily have given him a hundred. He was home.

But Laura wasn't. He rang and rang, then ran next door and down the concrete stairwell to the basement apartment. He rapped loudly on the door. Rosemary, the retired schoolteacher, looked a long time through the peephole before she began unspringing locks.

Laura was in Pennsylvania at Allenwood, seeing Douglas Muller about his parole. She told him this with one chain still on. Then, reluctantly, she undid that.

Allenwood was the minimum-security prison where the federal government interned nonviolent criminals. Douglas, one of Laura's clients, was a young Jesuit who had left the priesthood to oppose the draft without the shield of clerical status. The year before, when Zuckerman went down with Laura to visit him at the prison, Douglas confided to Nathan another reason for leaving: at Harvard, where the order had sent him to study Middle Eastern languages, he had lost his virginity. "That can happen," he said, "when you walk around Cambridge without your collar." Douglas wore the collar only when he was demonstrating for Cesar Chavez or against the war; otherwise he dressed in work shirts and jeans. He was a shy, thoughtful Midwesterner in his mid-twenties, the magnitude of whose devotion to the large self-denying cause was all in the ice-like clarity of his pale blue eyes.

Douglas knew something from Laura about

the novel Zuckerman was finishing and had amused the novelist, during his visit, with anecdotes about the hapless struggle he had waged as a high-school student against the sin of self-abuse. Grinning and blushing, he recalled for Zuckerman the days in Milwaukee when, having confessed first thing in the morning to the excesses of the night before, he was back in an hour to confess again. There was nothing in this world or the other that could help him, either; not the contemplation of Christ's passion, or the promise of the Resurrection, or the sympathetic priest at the Jesuit school who had in the end to refuse to give him absolution more than once every twenty-four hours. Recycled and fused with Nathan's own recollections, some of Douglas's best stories made their way into the life of Carnovsky, a budding soul no less bedeviled by onanism in Jewish New Jersey than Douglas growing up in Catholic Wisconsin. The inscribed first-edition copy of the book that the author sent to Allenwood had been acknowledged by the prisoner with a brief, compassionate note: "Tell poor Carnovsky that I pray for his strength. Fr. Douglas Muller."

"She'll be back tomorrow," Rosemary said

and waited by the door for Nathan to leave. She was acting as if he had bullied his way as far as the foyer and she intended him to trespass no farther.

In Rosemary's hall closet Laura kept her correspondence files. Guarding them from an F.B.I. break-in had given the lonely woman something to live for. So had Laura. For three years Laura had been mothering Rosemary like a daughter: accompanied her to the optometrist, took her to the hairdresser, weaned her from sleeping pills, baked the big cake for her seventieth birthday...

Zuckerman found he had to sit down, thinking of that endless list and the good woman who'd drawn it up.

Rosemary sat too, though she wasn't happy about it. Her chair was the Danish chair from his study, the old reading chair he had left behind. The battered Moroccan ottoman at her feet had also been his before the move uptown.

"How is your new apartment, Nathan?"

"Lonely. Very lonely."

She nodded as though he'd said "Fine." "And your work?"

"Work? Terrible. Nonexistent. Haven't worked in months."

"And how is your lovely mother?"

"God only knows."

Rosemary's hands had always trembled, and Zuckerman's answers weren't helping. She still looked like she could use a good meal. Sometimes Laura had come to sit with her when she had dinner, just to be sure she ate something.

"How's Laura, Rosemary?"

"Well, she's worried about young Douglas. She went again to Congressman Koch about his parole, but it doesn't look hopeful. His mood down there in the prison is not good."

"I wouldn't think so."

"This war is criminal. Unforgivable. I want to cry when I see what it is doing to the very best of our young men."

Laura had radicalized Rosemary—no mean job, either. Under the influence of her late bachelor brother, an Air Force colonel, Rosemary used to receive in her mailbox the publications of the John Birch Society; now she harbored Laura's files and worried about the welfare of her war resisters. And thought of Zuckerman as...as what? Did that matter to him too, Rosemary Ditson's judgment?

"How's Laura," he asked, "when she's not

worrying about Douglas? How is she managing otherwise?"

Rumor had reached him that three Movement higher-ups were pursuing Laura with great determination: a handsome philanthropist with an enormous social conscience, only recently divorced; a bearded civil-rights lawyer who could walk unaccompanied anywhere in Harlem, also recently divorced; and a burly, outspoken pacifist just back with Dave Dellinger from Hanoi, not yet married.

"You do her harm by telephoning her."

"Do I?"

She was holding the arms of her chair—his chair—to stop her hands from shaking. She wore two sweaters to keep herself warm and even in this mild May weather had a small electric heater burning by her side. Zuckerman remembered when Laura had gone out to buy it.

What she had to say wasn't easy for her, but she braced herself and got it out. "Why don't you realize that every time you leave your voice on her message machine it puts that poor girl back another two months!"

The uncharacteristic vehemence took him by surprise. "Does it? How?"

"You must not do this, Nathan. Please. You

abandoned her, that was your business. But now you must stop tormenting her and let her get on with her life. You call, after what you have done—please, let me finish—"

"Go ahead," he said, though he had made no effort to stop her.

"I don't want to go into it. I am only a neighbor. It's not my affair. Never mind."

"What isn't your affair?"

"Well—what you write in your books. Nor would you, with all your renown, listen to someone like me...But that you could do what you have done to Laura..."

"What is that?"

"The things you wrote about her in that book."

"About Laura? You don't mean Carnovsky's girlfriend, do you?"

"Don't hide behind that 'Carnovsky' business. Please don't compound it with that."

"I must say, Rosemary, I'm shocked to find that a woman who taught English in the New York school system for over thirty years cannot distinguish between the illusionist and the illusion. Maybe you're confusing the dictating ventriloquist with the demonic dummy."

"Don't hide behind sarcasm, either. I am old, but I am still a person."

"But do you really believe, you of all people, that the Laura we both know has anything in common with that woman portrayed in my book? Do you really believe that was what was going on next door between the two of us and the Xerox machine? That's exactly what *wasn't* going on."

Her head began to tremble a little, but she would not be put off. "I have no idea what you may have led her into. You are seven years her senior and an experienced man who has been married three times. You are a man who does not lack for imagination."

"Really, this is pretty foolish of you. Isn't it? It isn't as if you didn't know me too during these three years."

"I don't think I did, not now. I knew the polite you, the suave you, that's who I knew, Nathan. The charmer."

"The snake charmer."

"As you wish. I have read your book, if you want to know. As much as I could until my stomach turned. I am sure with all the publicity and all the money you can now find plenty of women of the kind you like. But Laura is out from under your spell, and you have no right to try to lure her back."

"You make me sound more like Svengali than Carnovsky."

"You plead on the phone, 'Laura, Laura, call me back,' and then she goes and reads the paper and finds this."

"Finds what?"

She handed him two clippings. They were right there on the table beside her chair.

I know, I know, actually you only want to know who's doing what to whom. Well, NATHAN ZUCKERMAN and CAESARA O'SHEA are still Manhattan's most delectable twosome. They were very together at the little dinner that agent ANDRE SCHEVITZ and wife MARY gave where KAY GRAHAM talked to WILLIAM STYRON and TONY RANDALL talked to LEONARD BERNSTEIN and LAUREN BACALL talked to GORE VIDAL and Nathan and Caesara talked to one another.

The second was groovier, if further from the circumstances as he remembered them.

Dancin' to Duchin at the Maisonette: Naughty Novelist Zuckerman, Sexy Superstar O'Shea...

"Is that the whole dossier?" he asked her. "Who was thoughtful enough to clip these out for Laura? You, Rosemary? I don't remember Laura herself taking an inordinate interest in the swinish press."

"With your education, with your lovely parents, with your wonderful talent for writing, with all that, to do what you have done to Laura—"

He got up to go. This was ridiculous. It was all ridiculous. Manhattan could as well have been another part of the forest, and his dignity handed over to Oberon and Puck. And handed to them by himself! To be taking to task this helpless old lady, to cast her as stand-in for everything driving him mad... surely, surely there was no need for him to go on.

"I assure you," he went on, "I have done absolutely nothing to harm Laura."

"Even you might speak differently if you still lived on this street and heard what I have to hear about that wonderful girl."

"Is that it? The gossips? Who? The florist? The grocer? The nice ladies in the pastry shop? Ignore 'em," he advised her, "just the way Laura does." He was surer of Laura than of himself. "I can't believe that I was born, even to my lovely parents, to provide moral reassurance to the grocer. Laura would agree."

"So that's how you do it," she said angrily. "You actually tell yourself that a young woman as fine as Laura has no feelings!"

Their conversation grew louder and more shameful and went on for another ten minutes. His world was getting stupider by the hour, and so was he.

She came to the window to watch him disappear forever from Laura's life. He mounted the concrete stairs and hurried away toward Abingdon Square. Then, at the corner, he doubled back and let himself into Laura's apartment. Their apartment. Five months, and he was still carrying the keys.

"Home!" he cried and raced for the bedroom.

Exactly as he'd left it! The anti-war posters, the post-impressionist posters, Laura's grandmother's patchwork quilt on the bed. That bed! All he had made of his indifference to her in that bed! As though he *were* Carnovsky with Carnovsky's obsession! As though, of all the readers infected by that book, the writer had had to go first. As though Rosemary were right and there'd been no illusion at all.

Next, the bathroom. There it was, the Xerox machine, third member in their ménage à trois. Taking a sheet of wastepaper from the trash basket beside the tub, he wrote on the clean side with his pen and ran off ten copies. "I LOVE YOU. PEACE NOW." But when he went with his leaflets into what once had been his study, he found a sleeping bag neatly laid out on the floor and a knapsack beside it stenciled "W.K." He had been expecting nothing, just the large barren room to which one day soon he would ship back his desk and his chair, and the four walls of empty shelves onto which he would realphabetize his books. But the shelves weren't entirely empty. Stacked on the shelf beside the sleeping bag were a dozen paperbacks. He picked through them, one by one: Dietrich Bonhoeffer, Simone Weil, Danilo Dolci, Albert Camus... He opened the closet where he used to store his reams of typing paper and hang his clothes. Empty, but for an unpressed gray jacket and a white shirt. He didn't notice the Roman collar until he took the shirt out and held it up to the light, ostensibly to see the size of his successor's neck.

217

A priest had taken his place. Father W.K.

He went into Laura's office to look at her perfectly ordered desk and her perfectly shelved books, and to see if he was wrong about the priest and if by chance his own photograph was still framed beside the phone. No. He tore up the leaflets intended for her "in" box and stuffed the pieces into his pocket. He would never have to worry about being bored by her again. A fallen man like himself he could perhaps have challenged, but he was no match for some saintly priest, undoubtedly yet another boy struggling against the forces of evil like Douglas Muller. Nor did he want to be around when Laura returned with Father W.K. from visiting Douglas at Allenwood Prison. How could they take seriously someone with his troubles? How could he?

He used her phone to call his answering service. The two of them had always to assume Laura's phone was tapped, but he for one had no secrets anymore: read all about it in Leonard Lyons. He just wanted to see if the kidnapper had called about the money, or if this time round Pepler had dropped the disguise.

Only one message, from his cousin Essie. *Urgent. Call me in Miami Beach at once.*

So it had happened, that morning, while he was out forgetting about it. While he was out pretending it was all some nutty prank of Alvin Pepler's! He couldn't stay in to wait for the kidnapper's phone call, he couldn't hang around, a man of his eminence, to be made a fool of yet again—and so instead it had happened. And to her. And because of him and his eminence and that character in that book!

And to *her*. Not to Carnovsky's mother, but to his own! And who was she, what was she, that such a thing should happen to *her?* Terrified of her tyrannical father, devoted to her lonely mother, the most loyal of wives to her demanding husband—oh, to her husband far more than that. Fidelity was nothing, fidelity she could give him with both hands tied behind her back. (He saw her hands bound with ropes, her mouth stuffed with a rag, her bare legs shackled to a stake in the ground.) How many nights had she sat through those stories of his impoverished childhood and never yawned, or groaned, or cried out, "Not you and Papa and the hat factory, not again." No, she knitted sweaters, she polished silver, she turned collars, and uncomplainingly, she heard about her husband's narrow escape

219

from the hat factory for the hundredth time. Once a year they quarreled. When the heavy winter rugs were taken up he tried to tell her how to roll them in the tar paper and the scene ended in shouting and tears. The husband shouting, the wife in tears. Otherwise, she never opposed him; however he did things was right.

That was the woman to whom this had happened.

Back when Henry was still in his carriage—this would be 1937—a truckdriver had whistled at her. It was summertime. She was sitting out front on the steps with the children. The truck slowed down, the driver whistled, and Zuckerman never forgot the milky smell of Henry's bottle wafting his way as he looked up from his tricycle to see her pulling her sundress over her knees and compressing her lips so as not to smile. At dinner that evening, when she told her husband the story, he leaned back in his chair and laughed. His wife a desirable woman? He was flattered. Men admiring her legs? Why not? They were legs to be proud of. Nathan, not quite five, was stunned; but not Dr. Zuckerman: any girl he'd married couldn't know the meaning of "to stray."

And to her, of all people, this had happened.

Once his mother went to a party with a flower in her hair. He must have been six or seven. It had taken him weeks to get over it.

And what else had she done to deserve this victimization?

Her youngest sister, Celia, had died in their house. She had come to recover from an operation. His mother walked Aunt Celia around the living room—he could to this day still see Celia, a frightening scarecrow in bathrobe and slippers, leaning feebly on his mother's arm. Aunt Celia had just graduated from normal school and was to be a music teacher in the Newark system. That, at any rate, was everyone's dream; she was the gifted girl in the family. But after the operation she couldn't even feed herself, let alone find strength in her hands to play chords on the piano. She couldn't make it from the breakfront to the radio without stopping to lean on the sofa, then the love seat, then his father's easy chair. But if they didn't drag her around the living room, she'd get pneumonia and die of that. "One more time, Celia dear, and that's it. A little bit every day," his mother told her, "and soon you'll be stronger.

Soon you'll be yourself again." After her walk Celia went listing back to the bed and his mother locked herself in the bathroom and cried. On weekends it was his father who walked her. "That's movin' along very nicely, Celia. That-a-girl." Softly, jauntily, with his dying young sister-in-law on his arm, Dr. Zuckerman whistled "I Can't Give You Anything but Love, Baby." He told everyone that at the funeral his wife "bore up like a soldier."

What did this woman understand of the savagery in people? How could she possibly endure it? Slice. Beat. Chop. Grind. Nowhere but in the kitchen did she run across such ideas. What violence she practiced went into making dinner. Otherwise, peace.

Her parents' daughter, her sister's sister, her husband's wife, her children's mother. What else was there? She would be the first to say "nothing." That was more than enough. Had taken all her *kayech,* her strength.

What strength would she have for this?

But she hadn't been kidnapped. It was his father: a coronary. "This is it," Essie told him. "You better hurry." When he got back to Eighty-first Street—to pack a bag before heading to Newark to meet his brother for the four o'clock Miami flight—a large manila envelope was dangling halfway out of his mailbox in the entryway. Weeks ago, after extracting an envelope, hand-delivered, addressed to "Kike, Apt. 2B," he had removed his nameplate from the box. In its place he had substituted a nameplate with his initials. Lately he had considered removing his initials and leaving the space blank, but he didn't because—because he refused to.

Across the envelope someone had scrawled with a red felt-tip pen, "Prestige Paté International." Inside was a damp matted handkerchief. It was the very one he'd given Pepler to dry his hands with the evening before, after Pepler had finished eating Zuckerman's sandwich. There was no note. Only, by way of a message, a stale acrid odor he had no difficulty identifying. Evidence, if evidence there need be, of the "hang-up" that Pepler shared with Gilbert Carnovsky, and that Zuckerman had stolen from him for that book.

4

Look Homeward, Angel

On the table beside the bed were five-cent Xerox copies of every page of every protest letter Dr. Zuckerman had mailed to Lyndon Johnson while he was President. In contrast to his collected letters to Hubert Humphrey, the Johnson folder, bound with a wide rubber band, was nearly as fat as *War and Peace*. The sparsity and brevity of the Humphrey letters—also their sarcasm, their abusive bitterness—showed how far he had sunk in Dr. Zuckerman's esteem since he'd been the darling of the A.D.A. Most days Humphrey had gotten no more than one line of contempt and three exclamation marks. And on a post-card, so that anybody who picked it up could learn what a coward the Vice-President had

become. But with the President of the United
States, arrogant pig-headed bastard though
he was, Dr. Zuckerman had tried to be reasonable on letterhead stationery, invoking the
name of F.D.R. at every opportunity, and elu-
cidating his argument against the war with
wisdom, not always assigned with the utmost
scrupulosity, from either the Talmud or a
long-deceased spinster named Helen Mac-
Murphy. Miss MacMurphy, as all the family
knew (as all the world knew, from the title
story of *Higher Education,* Nathan Zuckerman, 1959), had been his eighth-grade teacher.
In 1912 she had gone to Dr. Zuckerman's
father, a sweatshop worker, to demand that
bright little Victor be sent to high school instead of into the local hat factory, where an
older brother was already crippling his fingers
working as a blocker fourteen hours a day.
And as all the world knew, she had prevailed.

Though Lyndon Johnson turned out to
have neither the time nor—in Mrs. Zuckerman's phrase—"the common decency" to
respond to the letters he received from the
lifelong Democrat ailing in Florida, Dr. Zuckerman went on dictating some three or four
pages to his wife just about every other day,
lecturing the President on American history,
226

Jewish history, and his own personal philosophy. After the stroke that had wrung all coherence from his speech, he seemed not to have any idea what was going on in his room, let alone in the Oval Office, where his archenemy Nixon was now ruining things; but then slow improvement began once again—his will, the doctors told Mrs. Zuckerman, was a wonder to them. Mr. Metz came to visit and to read aloud to him from *The New York Times,* and then one afternoon Dr. Zuckerman managed to communicate to his wife that he wanted his correspondence folders brought to him from the table beside the wheelchair at home. She would, after this, sit there by his side and turn the sheets of paper, so he could see all he had once written and would live to write again. At his request, she began to show the letters to the doctors and nurses who stopped by his bed to attend him. He was regaining his clarity, he was even beginning to demonstrate some of his old "fire," when one day, only moments after Mr. Metz had left, just as Mrs. Zuckerman had arrived to take up the afternoon shift, he dropped into unconsciousness and had to be rushed to the hospital. Mrs. Zuckerman found herself inside the ambulance with the correspondence folders in her hands. "Anything, anything," she said, explaining her state of mind to Nathan later, "anything to give him the will to go on." Zuckerman wondered if to herself, at least, she was able to say, "Enough, let it be over. I can't endure his enduring like this anymore."

But then, she was the wife whose every thought the man had been thinking for her since she was twenty years old, not the son who'd been fighting his every thought since he was younger even than that. In the plane flying down, Zuckerman had been remembering the summer just twenty years ago, that August before he'd left for college, when he read three thousand pages of Thomas Wolfe straight through on the screened-in back porch of his family's stifling home—stifling that August as much because of the father as of the weather. "He believed himself thus at the center of life; he believed the mountains rimmed the heart of the world; he believed that from all the chaos of accident the inevitable event came at the inexorable moment to add to the sum of his life." Inevitable. Inexorable. "Oh yes!" noted stifled Nathan in the margin of his copy of *Look Homeward, Angel,* unaware that the resounding privative clang of the Latinate adjectives wasn't necessarily so stirring when you ran into the inevitable and the inexorable at the center of your life instead of on the back porch. All he wanted at sixteen was to become a romantic genius like Thomas Wolfe and leave little New Jersey and all the shallow provincials therein for the deep emancipating world of Art. As it turned out, he had taken them all with him.

Zuckerman's father got "better" and then worse again all through the first night Nathan was there, and most of the following day. Sometimes when he came to, he seemed to his wife to be inclining his head toward the letters in the folder beside the bed; she took this to mean that he had something in mind to tell the new President. Inasmuch, thought Zuckerman, as he still had a mind. She wasn't making much sense anymore herself—she'd had no sleep for over twenty-four hours, and little during the four preceding years—and finally it was easier than not for Zuckerman to pretend that she might be right. He drew a yellow pad out of his briefcase and printed in large letters "STOP THE WAR"; below it, in his own hand, he signed "Dr. Victor Zuckerman." But when he showed the page to his father it evoked no response. Dr. Zuckerman made sounds from time to time, but they were barely distinguishable as words. They were more like the squeals of a mouse. It was awful.

At dusk, after Dr. Zuckerman had again been unconscious for several hours, the resident took Nathan aside and told him it would be over in a few hours. He would silently slip away, the doctor said, but then the doctor didn't know Nathan's father the way the family did. In fact, near the end, as sometimes happens to you if you're lucky—or unlucky— the dying man opened his eyes and seemed suddenly to see them all and to see them together, and to understand as well as anyone in that room exactly what was up. This was awful too, another way. It was more awful. His soft, misty gaze somehow grew enormous, bending their images and drawing them to him like a convex mirror. His chin was quivering—not from the frustrated effort of speech but from the recognition that all effort was pointless now. And it had been the most effortful life. Being Victor Zuckerman was no job you took lightly. Day shifts, night shifts, weekends, evenings, vacations—for sheer

man-hours, not so different from being his
son.

Gathered around him, when he came to,
were Henry, Nathan, their mother, Cousin
Essie, and the newcomer to the family, Essie's
kindly, genial husband Mr. Metz, a retired
accountant of seventy-five, who stood be-
nignly apart from their ancient entangle-
ments, reproaching no one for anything and
thinking mostly about playing bridge. Each
was only to have stayed with Dr. Zuckerman
for five minutes, but because Nathan was
Nathan, hospital rules had been suspended
by the physician in charge.

They all closed in to look down at that terrified, imploring gaze. Essie, at seventy-four
still nobody to tamper with, took hold of his
hand and began reminiscing about the winepress in the cellar of the house on Mercer
Street, and how all the cousins used to love
to watch Dr. Zuckerman's father crush the
Concord grapes there in the fall. She had as
big and commanding a voice as ever, and
when she moved on from Victor's father's
winepress to Victor's mother's mandel bread,
a nurse came to the open door with a finger
to her lips to remind Essie that people were
sick.

Tucked way down into the bed sheets, Dr. Zuckerman could have been a frightened four-year-old listening to a story to put him to sleep, but for his mustache, and what three strokes and a coronary had done to his face. His gray, imploring eyes looked steadily back at Essie as she recalled how the century had begun for the new family in America. Was it getting through to him—the old winepress, the new American children, the sweet-smelling cellar, the crunchy mandel bread, and the mother, the revered and simple mother who baked the mandel bread? Suppose he could remember it all, every cherished sensation that had been his in the life he was leaving—was that necessarily the easiest way to go? Having buried her share, maybe Essie knew what she was doing. Not that not knowing had ever worried her before. Precious time was passing, but Essie wasn't one to stint on details, nor did Nathan see any way to stop her now that she had the floor. Besides, he couldn't hold anyone in check anymore—he couldn't hold himself in check anymore. After a day and a half, he was finally in tears. There were tubes to deliver oxygen to his father's lungs, tubes to drain the urine from his bladder, tubes to drip dextrose into his veins, and none of them would make the least difference. For several minutes it was he who felt like the four-year-old, discovering for the first time how utterly helpless his protector could be.

"Remember Uncle Markish, Victor?"

From Essie's vantage point, the homeless rascal Markish had been the family character; from Dr. Zuckerman's (and his older son's—cf. "Higher Education"), it had been Essie. Uncle Markish painted their houses and slept on their stairwells, and then picked up and went off one day in his coveralls to Shanghai, China. "You'll wind up like Markish," was what they would tell the children in that clan who came home from school with any grade lower than B. If you wanted to leave Jersey for China, you did it through the Oriental Studies Department of a top-flight school and not with nothing to your name but a paint bucket and brush. In their family either you did things right, preferably as a D.D.S. or an M.D. or an L.L.B. or a Ph.D., or you might as well not do them at all. Law laid down by the son of the toiling, uncomplaining mother who made the mandel bread and the driven, impregnable father who pressed the wine.

On the airplane down, Zuckerman had read through an illustrated paperback for laymen about the creation of the universe and the evolution of life. The author was a NASA scientist who had lately achieved celebrity by explaining elementary astronomy once a week on public television. Zuckerman bought the book off a rack at Newark Airport after meeting Henry for the flight to Miami. There were books from his boxes that might have meant more to him on his way to see his father die, but he couldn't get at them and so left the apartment for Newark empty-handed. What did those books have to do with his father anyway? If they'd ever meant to his father what the discovery of them had meant at school to him, it would have been another household, another childhood, another life. So, instead of thinking the thoughts of the great thinkers on the subject of death, he thought his own. There were more than enough for a three-hour flight: plans for his mother's future, memories of his father's life, the origin of his own mixed emotions. *Mixed Emotions* had been the title of his second book. It had confused his father no less than *Higher Education*, his first. Why should emotions be mixed? They weren't when he was a boy.

Zuckerman had reached Henry just as he'd gotten back to the office from a conference in Montreal. He hadn't heard the news, and when Zuckerman gave it to him—"This looks like it"—Henry emitted the most wrenching sob. Another reason Zuckerman wouldn't be needing anything inspirational to read on the flight down. He had a kid brother to tend to, emotionally more fragile than he liked to let on.

But Henry arrived at the airport looking nothing like a kid, in a dark pinstriped suit and carrying in his monogrammed briefcase the back issues of a dental journal he meant to catch up on. And so Zuckerman, a little let down at not having to buck him up, and a little amused at feeling a little let down—stunned a little, too, that he should have been expecting a ten-year-old child to be in his charge flying south—Zuckerman wound up reading about the origin of everything.

As a result, when it was his turn to say goodbye to his father, he did not hark back to Grandma's mandel bread. Grandma's mandel bread had been wonderful enough, but

Essie had covered it as thoroughly as anyone ever could, and so instead Zuckerman explained to him the big-bang theory, as he'd come to understand it the day before. He would try to get through to him how long things had been burning up and burning out: maybe it would get through to the family as well. It wasn't just a father who was dying, or a son, or a cousin, or a husband: it was the whole creation, whatever comfort that gave.

Back before Grandma's mandel bread then. Before even Grandma.

"I was reading on the plane about the beginning of the universe. Dad, do you hear me?"

"He hears, don't worry," said Essie. "He hears everything now. He's never missed a trick in his life. Right, Victor?"

"Not the world," said Nathan, to his father's searching eyes, "but the universe. Scientists now believe it began between ten and twenty billion years ago."

His hand rested lightly on his father's arm. It seemed impossible—there was nothing to that arm anymore. As little children the Zuckerman boys would watch with delight while their father pretended to inflate his biceps by blowing air in through his thumbs.

236

Well, they were gone now, Papa's Popeye biceps, vanished like the primordial egg of hydrogen energy in which the universe was conceived... Yes, in spite of a growing sense that he was engaged in a flagrant act of pretentious, useless, professorial foolishness, Zuckerman lectured on: the original egg that one fine day, reaching a temperature of thousands of billions of degrees, blew itself wide open, and like an erupting furnace forged on the spot all the elements that would ever be. "All of this," he informed his father, "in the first half hour of that very first day."

Dr. Zuckerman registered no surprise. Why should he? What was the first half hour of the first day of Creation to the last half hour of the last day of his life?

Oh, the mandel bread was a much better idea. Homely, tangible, and to the point of Victor Zuckerman's real life and a Jewish family deathbed scene. But the oration on mandel bread was Essie being Essie, and this, however foolish, was himself being himself. Proceed, Nathan, to father the father. Last chance to tell the man what he still doesn't know. Last chance ever to make him see it all another way. You'll change him yet.

"—the universe expanding outward ever

since, the galaxies all rushing away, out into space, from the impact of that first big bang. And it will go on like this, the universe blowing outward and outward, for fifty billion years."

No response here, either.

"Go on, he's listening." Essie, giving instructions.

"I'm afraid," he told her softly, "it's hard enough to grasp when you're on top of the world—"

"Don't worry about it. Go on. This family has always been smarter than you think."

"I grant that, Esther. It's my stupidity I was thinking about."

"Talk to *him,* Nathan." It was his mother, in tears. "Essie, I beg you, let sleeping dogs lie, at least tonight."

Nathan looked across the bed to Henry. His brother had a tight hold on one of his father's hands, but he too was running with tears and didn't look in any shape to say anything by way of farewell. The inexpressible love breaking out, or the blockaded hatred? Henry was the good son, but it didn't come cheap, or so Zuckerman was inclined to believe. Henry was the tallest, darkest, and handsomest by far of all the Zuckerman men, a swarthy, virile, desert Zuckerman whose genes, uniquely for their clan, seemed to have traveled straight from Judea to New Jersey without the Diaspora detour. He had a light, mellifluous voice, and the most kindly, gentle, doctorly manner, and invariably his patients fell in love with him. And he fell in love with some of his patients. Zuckerman alone knew this. Some two years earlier Henry had driven to New York in the middle of the night prepared to sleep in Nathan's study in Nathan's pajamas because he could not bear any longer to sleep in the same bed with his wife. Watching Carol undress for bed had caused him to remember (not that he had reason to forget) the body of the patient whom he had himself undressed only a few hours earlier in a north Jersey motel, and he fled to New York at two a.m., without even taking time to pull socks on under his loafers. He sat up all night telling his big brother about his mistress, sounding to Zuckerman like some miserable, yearning, tenderized lover out of the great nineteenth-century literature of adultery.

Henry was still talking at seven a.m. when Carol had phoned. She didn't know what she'd done wrong and begged him to come home. Zuckerman picked up the extension to

listen in. Henry was crying and Carol was
pleading. "—you wanted plants like your
grandmother had in her living room, I gave
you plants. One day you said something about
having had eggs in an eggcup as a kid on a
vacation in Lakewood—the next morning I
presented your boiled egg to you in an eggcup.
And you were *like* a kid, so sweet, so delighted, so content from such a little thing.
You couldn't wait until Leslie was old enough
so you could begin to call him 'son.' You *didn't*
wait. You used to lie on the floor with him
and let him chew on your ear and you were
in seventh heaven. You used to call out the
door when dinner was ready, 'Son, come on
home, time to eat.' You did it with Ruthie.
You still do it with Ellen. You rush to do it
when I say the food is ready. 'Little girl, come
on, supper.' Ruthie plays 'Twinkle, Twinkle,
Little Star' on her violin, and you, you fool,
you're in tears, you're so happy. Leslie tells
you that everything is made out of molecules,
and you're so proud you're repeating it all
night to anybody who calls. Oh, Henry, you
are the softest, gentlest, kindest, most touching man there is, in your heart you are really
the simplest man in the world to satisfy—"

So Henry went home.

Softest, gentlest, kindest. Responsibility. Generosity. Devotion. That's how everybody spoke of Henry. I suppose if I were Henry with his heart I wouldn't jeopardize it, either. It probably feels very good being so good. Except when it doesn't. And that probably feels good in the end too. Self-sacrifice.

They were no longer the brothers they'd once been.

A hand came gently down on Nathan's shoulder—Essie's dapper, tanned, well-meaning husband. "Finish the story," said Mr. Metz softly. "You're telling it beautiful."

He had stopped to watch his emotional brother, but now he smiled and assured Mr. Metz that he would go on. It was the first time that Mr. Metz had ever referred to anything of Zuckerman's as a "story." Zuckerman's short stories he called articles. "Your mother showed me your article in the magazine. Excellent, excellent." He was famous for buttering everyone up, Essie for tearing them down. They were an act Zuckerman always tried to take in when he flew to see his parents in Florida. With his father as a third they could have gone on tour: Dr. Zuckerman was famous for fanatical devotion. F.D.R. topped the list, followed by Mrs. Roosevelt,

Harry Truman, David Ben-Gurion, and the authors of *Fiddler on the Roof*.

"You are their wordsmith," Mr. Metz whispered. "You are their mouthpiece. You can say for everyone what is in their hearts."

He turned back to his father: no closer to death, though just as far from life. "Dad, listen to me, if you can." For whatever it was worth, Nathan smiled at him too. Last smile. "Dad, there's now a theory . . . if you can follow me."

Essie: "He can follow you."

"There is now a theory that when the fifty billion years are up, instead of everything coming to an end, instead of all the light going out because of all the energy fizzling away, gravity will take over. The force of gravity," he repeated, as though it were the familiar name of one of the beloved grandchildren up in South Orange. "Just at the edge of the end, the whole thing will begin to contract, will begin to rush back toward the center. Do you follow me? This too will take fifty billion years, until it's all pulled down inside that original egg, into this compressed droplet that it all began with. And there, you see, heat and energy build up again, and bang, another stupendous explosion, and out it'll all go flying, a brand-new roll of the dice, a brand-new creation unlike any that's been. If the theory is correct, the universe will go on like this forever. If it's correct—and I want you to hear this, this is what I want you to listen to very carefully, this is what we all want to tell you—"

"That's the ticket," said Mr. Metz.

"If it's correct, the universe *has* been going on forever: fifty billion years out, fifty billion years back. Imagine it. A universe being reborn and reborn and reborn, without end."

He did not, at this point, report to his father the objection to this theory as he had understood it on the plane ride down, a considerable objection, a crushing objection really, having to do with the density of matter in the universe being marginally insufficient for the friendly, dependable force of gravity to take over and halt the expansion before the last of the fires went out. If not for this insufficiency, the whole thing might indeed oscillate to and fro without end. But according to the paperback still in his coat pocket, right now they couldn't find what they needed anywhere, and the chances for no ending didn't look good.

But this information his father could live

without. Of all that Dr. Zuckerman had so far lived without, and that Nathan would have preferred for him to live *with,* knowledge of the missing density factor was the least of it. Enough for now of what is and isn't so. Enough science, enough art, enough of fathers and sons.

A major new development in the life of Nathan and Victor Zuckerman, but then the coronary-care unit of Miami Biscayne Hospital isn't the Goddard Institute for Space Studies, as anyone who's ever been there doesn't have to be told.

Though Dr. Zuckerman didn't officially expire until the next morning, it was here that he uttered his last words. Word. Barely audible, but painstakingly pronounced. "Bastard," he said.

Meaning who? Lyndon Johnson? Hubert Humphrey? Richard Nixon? Meaning He who had not seen fit to bestow upon His own universe that measly bit of missing matter, that one lousy little hydrogen atom for each volume of ten cubic feet? Or to bestow upon Dr. Zuckerman, ardent moralist from grade school on, the simple reward of a healthy old age and a longer life? But then, when he spoke his last, it wasn't to his correspondence fold-

ers that he was looking, or upward at the face
of his invisible God, but into the eyes of the
apostate son.

The funeral was a tremendous strain. There
was the heat, for one thing. Over the Miami
cemetery, the sun made its presence known
to Zuckerman as no Yahweh ever had; had
it been the sun they were all addressing, he
might have entered into the death rites of his
people with something more than just respect
for his mother's feelings. The two sons had to
support her between them from the moment
they left the air-conditioned limousine and
started down between a row of twirling sprin-
klers to the burial plot. Dr. Zuckerman had
bought two plots, for himself and for his wife,
six years earlier, the same week he'd bought
their condominium in Harbor Beach Retirement Village. Her knees gave way by the
grave, but as she had been worn down by her
husband's illness to little more than a hundred
pounds, it was no problem for Henry and Nathan to keep her on her feet until the coffin
was lowered and they could take refuge from
the heat. Behind him, Zuckerman heard Essie tell Mr. Metz, "All the words, all the ser-

mons, all the quotations, and no matter what they say, it's still final." Earlier, stepping from the limousine, she had turned to Zuckerman to give her assessment of the journey out for the man in the hearse. "You take a ride and you don't get to see the scenery." Yes, Essie and he were the ones who'd say anything.

Zuckerman, his brother, and the rabbi were, by decades, the youngest men present. The rest of them wilting there were either his parents' elderly neighbors from Harbor Beach or Newark cronies of his father's who'd also retired to Florida. A few had even been boys with Dr. Zuckerman in the Central Ward before the First World War. Most of them Zuckerman hadn't seen since his childhood, when they'd been men not much older than he was now. He listened to the familiar voices coming out of the lined and jowled and fallen faces, thinking, If only I were still writing *Carnovsky*. What memories those tones touched off—the Charlton Street baths and the Lakewood vacations, the fishing expeditions to the Shark River inlet down the shore! Before the funeral everybody had come up to put their arms around him. Nobody mentioned the book; probably none of them had read it. Of all the obstacles in life that these retired salesmen and merchants and manufacturers had struggled with and overcome, reading through a book was not yet one. Just as well. Not even the young rabbi made mention of *Carnovsky* to the author. Perhaps out of respect for the dead. All the better. He was not there as "the author"—the author was back in Manhattan. Here he was Nathan. Sometimes life offers no more powerful experience than just such a divestment.

He recited the Mourners' Kaddish. Over a sinking coffin, even a nonbeliever needs some words to chant, and *"Yisgadal v'yiskadash..."* made more sense to him than "Rage against the dying of the light." If ever there was a man to bury as a Jew it was his father. Nathan would probably wind up letting them bury him as one too. Better as that than as a bohemian.

"My two boys," said his mother, as they lifted her along the path back to the car. "My two tall strong handsome boys."

Returning through Miami to the apartment, the limousine stopped for a light just by a supermarket; the women shoppers, most of them middle-aged and Cuban, were wearing halters and shorts, and high-heeled sandals. A lot of protoplasm to take in straight from the post-retirement village of the dead. He saw Henry looking too. A halter had always seemed to Zuckerman a particularly provocative piece of attire—cloth not quite clothing—but the only thought inspired by these women oozing flesh was of his father decomposing. He'd been unable to think of much else since earlier in the day when the family had taken seats together in the first row at the Temple and the young rabbi— bearded very like Che Guevara—began to extol from the altar the virtues of the deceased. The rabbi praised him not simply as father, husband, and family man, but as "a political being engaged by all of life and anguished by the suffering of mankind." He spoke of the many magazines and newspapers Dr. Zuckerman had subscribed to and studied, the countless letters of protest he had painstakingly composed, he spoke of his enthusiasm for American democracy, his passion for Israel's survival, his revulsion against the carnage in Vietnam, his fears for the Jews in the Soviet Union, and meanwhile all Zuckerman was thinking was the word "extinguished." All that respectable moralizing, all that repressive sermonizing, all those superfluous prohibitions, that furnace of pieties, that Lucifer of rectitude, that Hercules of misunderstanding, extinguished.

Strange. It was supposed to be just the opposite. But never had he contemplated his father's life with less sentiment. It was as though they were burying the father of some other sons. As for the character being depicted by the rabbi, well, nobody had ever gotten Dr. Zuckerman quite so wrong. Maybe the rabbi was only trying to distance him from the father in *Carnovsky,* but from the portrait he painted you would have thought Dr. Zuckerman was Schweitzer. All that was missing was the organ and the lepers. But why not? Whom did it harm? It was a funeral, not a novel, let alone the Last Judgment.

What made it such a strain? Aside from the unrelenting heat and their lost, defenseless, seemingly legless mother? Aside from the pitiful sight of those old family friends, looking down into the slot where they too must be deposited, thirty, sixty, ninety days hence—the kibitzing giants out of his earliest memories, so frail now, some of them, that despite the healthy suntans, you could have pushed them in with his father and they couldn't have crawled out...? Aside from all

249

this, there were his emotions. The strain of feeling no grief. The surprise. The shame. The exultation. The shame of that. But all the grieving over his father's body had taken place when Nathan was twelve and fifteen and twenty-one: the grief over all his father had been dead to while living. From that grief the death was a release.

By the time he boarded the Newark plane with Henry, it felt like a release from even more. He couldn't entirely explain—or manage to control—this tide of euphoria sweeping him away from all inane distractions. It was very likely the same heady feeling of untrammeled freedom that people like Mary and André had been expecting him to enjoy from becoming a household name. In fact it had rather more to do with the four-day strain of Florida, with the wholly un-inane exigencies of arranging for the burial of one parent and the survival of the other, that had put the household name and the Hallelujah Chorus behind him. He had become himself again—though with something unknowable added: he was no longer any man's son. Forget fathers, he told himself. Plural.

Forget kidnappers too. During the four days away, his answering service had taken no message from either an ominous palooka or an addled Alvin Pepler. Had his *landsman* spent into Zuckerman's handkerchief the last of his enraged and hate-filled adoration? Was that the end of this barrage? Or would Zuckerman's imagination beget still other Peplers conjuring up novels out of his—novels disguising themselves as actuality itself, as nothing less than real? Zuckerman the stupendous sublimator spawning Zuckermaniacs! A book, a piece of fiction bound between two covers, breeding living fiction exempt from all the subjugations of the page, breeding fiction unwritten, unreadable, unaccountable and uncontainable, instead of doing what Aristotle promised from art in Humanities 2 and offering moral perceptions to supply us with the knowledge of what is good or bad. Oh, if only Alvin had studied Aristotle with him at Chicago! If only he could understand that it is the writers who are supposed to move the readers to pity and fear, not the other way around!

He had never so enjoyed a takeoff in his life. He let his knees fall open and, as the plane went gunning like a hot rod down the runway, felt the driving level force of the fuselage as though it were his own. And when it lifted off—lifted like some splendid, ostentatious afterthought—Zuckerman suddenly pictured Mussolini hanging by his heels. He'd never forgotten that photograph on the front page of the papers. Who could, of his generation of American youngsters? But to remember the vengeful undoing of that vile tyrant after the death of your own law-abiding, anti-Fascist, nonviolent father, chief air-raid warden of Keer Avenue and lifetime champion of the B'nai B'rith Anti-Defamation League? Reminder to the outer man of the inner man he's dealing with.

Of course for some seventy-two hours now he had been wondering if his father's last word could really have been "Bastard." Under the strain of that long vigil his hearing may not have been too subtle. Bastard? To mean what? *You were never my real son.* But was this father equal to such unillusioned thought, ever? Though maybe that's what he read in my eyes: *Henry's your boy, Papa, not me.* But from my two eyes? No, no, some things I'm not unillusioned enough for either, out of the safety of the study. Maybe he just said "Faster." Telling Death his job the way he told his wife how to roll the winter rugs and Henry how to do homework when he dawdled.

252

"Vaster"? Unlikely. Nathan's cosmology lecture notwithstanding, for his father, in dying as in living, there were still but two points of reference in all the vastness: the family and Hitler. You could do worse, but you could also do better. Better. Of course! Not "Bastard" but "Better." First principle, final precept. Not more light but more virtue. He had only been reminding them to be better boys. "Bastard" was the writer's wishful thinking, if not quite the son's. Better scene, stronger medicine, a final repudiation by Father. Still, when Zuckerman wasn't writing he was also only human, and he'd just as soon the scene wasn't so wonderful. Kafka once wrote, "I believe that we should read only those books that bite and sting us. If a book we are reading does not rouse us with a blow to the head, then why read it?" Agreed, as to books. But as for life, why invent a blow to the head where none was intended? Up with art, but down with mythomania.

Mythomania? Alvin Pepler. The very word is like a bell that tolls thee back to me.

That Pepler's credentials were in order—if nothing else—Essie had confirmed for Zuckerman the night after the funeral, when everyone else had gone to sleep. The two were in her kitchen eating the remains of the cinnamon cake served the guests earlier in the day. For as long as Zuckerman could remember, Essie was supposed to be eating herself into an early grave. Also smoking herself to death. She was one of many his father could always find time to lecture about the right way to live. "He used to sit at the window," Essie told Nathan, "sit there in that wheelchair and call down to the people parking their cars. They didn't park right to suit him. Just yesterday I ran into a woman who your mother is still afraid to talk to because of your old man. Old Mrs. Oxburg. She is from Cincinnati, a multimillionairess ten times over. When your little mother spots her coming, she runs the other way. One day Victor saw Mrs. Oxburg sitting in the lobby by an air conditioner, minding her own business, and he told her to move, she was going to give herself pneumonia. She said to him, 'Please, Dr. Zuckerman, where I sit is none of your business.' But, no, he wouldn't accept that for an answer. Instead he started telling her how our little cousin Sylvia died in 1918 of influenza, and how beautiful and smart she was, and what it did to Aunt Gracie. Your mother couldn't stop him. Whenever she tried just wheeling him away, he threw a fit. She had to go to the doctor to get Valium, and the Valium I had to keep for her here because if he found it he would start shouting at her about becoming a drug addict."

"He went a little over the top in that chair, Essie. We all know that."

"Poor Hubert Humphrey. I pity that poor bastard, if he read your father's postal cards. What the hell could Humphrey do, Nathan? He wasn't President, Vietnam wasn't his idea. He was as flummoxed as the next guy. But you couldn't tell that to Victor."

"Well, Humphrey's torment's over now."

"So is Victor's."

"That too."

"Okay, Nathan—let's move on. You and me are not lilies of the valley. This is my chance to get the dirt, and without your mother in between, making believe you still use your little putz just to run water through. I want to hear about you and the movie star. What happened? You dropped her or she dropped you?"

"I'll tell you all about the movie star, first tell me about the Peplers."

"From Newark? With the son, you mean? Alvin?"

"Right. Alvin from Newark. What do you have on him?"

"Well, he was on television. They had those quiz programs, remember? I think he won twenty-five grand. He had a big write-up in the *Star-Ledger*. This is years ago already. He was in the Marines before that. Didn't they award him a Purple Heart? I think he got it in the head. Maybe it was the foot. Anyway, when he came on they used to play 'From the Halls of Montezuma' in his honor. What do you want to know about him for?"

"I ran into him in New York. He introduced himself on the street. I would say from our meeting that it was the head, not the foot."

"Oh yeah? A screwball? Well, he was supposed to know his Americana inside out—that's how he won the dough. But of course they gave them the answers anyway. That was the big scandal. For a while he was all anybody in Newark talked about. I went to high school with his Aunt Lottie back in the year one, so I followed every week how he came out. Look, everybody did. Then he lost and that was that. Now he's nuts?"

"A little, I thought."

"Well, that's what they tell me about you, you know. And not just a little."

"What do you tell them?"

"I say it's true. I say he has to wear a strait-jacket all the way to the bank. That shuts them up. How about the movie star? Who dumped who?"

"I dumped her."

"Idiot. She's gorgeous and must be worth a fortune. For Christ's sake, Nathan, why?"

"She's gorgeous and worth a fortune, but not of our faith, Esther."

"I don't remember that stopping you before. I thought, myself, it egged you on. So who are you driving wild now?"

"Golda Meir."

"Oh, you're a sly little fox, Nathan, behind those harmless professor's glasses. You were always taking it in, even as a kid. There was your brother, the goody-good patrol boy who never stayed up past his bedtime, and there was you, thinking to yourself what a bunch of stupid bastards we all were. Still, I have to hand it to you, you have put something over on the public with this book. If I were you, I wouldn't listen to one goddamn thing they say."

The seat-belt sign had flashed off, and Henry

had tilted his seat back and was sipping the
martini he'd ordered at takeoff. He was
hardly what you'd call a drinking man, and
in fact was taking down the martini like a
slightly noxious medicinal preparation. His
complexion seemed somehow darkly sickish
that morning—rather than darkly romantic—as though cinders had been ground into
his skin. Zuckerman couldn't remember seeing
his brother so emotionally done in since a
weekend thirteen years before, when he'd
come down from Cornell as a sophomore and
announced he was giving up chemistry to become a "drama major." He was fresh from
appearing as the Ragpicker in *The Madwoman of Chaillot*. Henry had gotten the lead
role in the first college production he'd tried
out for, and now he spoke with reverence at
the dinner table of the two new influences on
his life: John Carradine, who had played the
Ragpicker on Broadway, and whom he hoped
to emulate on the stage (in appearance as
well—he'd already lost ten pounds trying),
and Timmy, the young student director of the
Cornell *Madwoman*. Timmy had painted flats
the summer before in Provincetown, where
his parents had a vacation house. Timmy was
sure he could get Henry work there too, "in
258

stock." "And when is this?" asked Mrs. Zuckerman, who was still abashed at why he'd gotten so thin. "Timmy says next summer," answered Henry. "Next June." "And what about the Chernicks?" his father asked. The previous two summers Henry had worked as a waterfront counselor for two Newark gym-teacher brothers who owned a camp for Jewish children in the Adirondacks. The job had come to someone as young as Henry as a special favor from the Chernicks to his father. "What about your responsibility to Lou and Buddy Chernick?" he was asked. In the way of vulnerable, ceremonious, intelligent children who all their lives have been delivering obedience in the form of streaming emotion, Henry couldn't give his father the kind of answer he might have come up with in a course in ethics—he ran from the table instead. Because all the way down from Ithaca he'd been expecting the worst—because for three days he'd been unable to eat, in dread of this very meal—he collapsed before it even got half as bad as he'd predicted it would to Timmy. The two boys had for days rehearsed the scene together in their dorm, Timmy playing Dr. Zuckerman like a miniature Lear, and Henry as a rather outspoken ver-

sion of himself—Henry playing at being Nathan.

Only three hours into the visit, and Nathan
had to be phoned in Manhattan—secretly,
and tearfully, by his mother—and told to
come right home to make peace between the
Ragpicker and his father. Carrying messages
back and forth between Henry—locked in his
bedroom quoting Timmy and Sinclair Lewis's
Babbitt—and his father—in the living room
enumerating the opportunities denied to him
in 1918 that life was now offering to Henry
on a silver platter—Nathan was able to
negotiate a settlement by three a.m. All decisions about Henry's career were to be post-
poned for twelve months. He could continue
to act in student plays but at the same time
he must continue to carry on as a chemistry
major and to fulfill his "obligation," if only
for one more summer, to the Chernicks. Then,
next year, they would all sit down together
to reassess the situation...a meeting that
never took place, because by the following fall
Henry was engaged to Carol Goff, a girl
judged by Henry's father to have "a head on
her shoulders," and no more was heard of
John Carradine or of Timmy, either. *Timmy!*
The young drama student's Christian name

couldn't have sounded more Christian, or more seditious, as enunciated by their father in the heat of the fray. During that memorable Friday-night family battle back in 1956, Nathan had himself dared to counter at one point with the sacred name of Paul Muni, but *"Timmy!"* his father cried, like a war whoop, *"Timmy!"* and Nathan saw that not even Paul Muni as wily Clarence Darrow, not even Paul Muni live in their living room as patient Louis Pasteur could have persuaded Dr. Zuckerman that a Jew in pancake makeup on the stage was probably no more or less ridiculous in the eyes of God than a Jew in a dental smock drilling a tooth. Then Henry met sweet and studious Carol Goff, a scholarship girl, and gave her his ZBT pin— and so the argument ended for good. Zuckerman figured that was why he'd given her the pin, though officially, he knew, it was to commemorate the loss of Carol's virginity earlier that night. When Henry tried the next semester to get the pin back, it so upset Carol and her family that two weeks later Henry changed his mind and got engaged to Carol instead. And, in their senior year, the upshot of Henry gently trying to break the engagement was their marriage the month after

graduation. No, Henry simply couldn't bear
to see this kindly, thoughtful, devoted, harmless, self-sacrificing creature suffering so, and
suffering so over him. He couldn't bear to
make anybody who loved him suffer. He
couldn't be that selfish or that cruel.

In the days after the funeral, Henry had
several times simply begun to sob in the middle of a conversation—in the middle of a sentence having nothing even to do with the
death of their father—and in order to collect
himself, went out to take a long walk alone.
One morning only minutes after Henry had
fled the apartment, unshaven and again close
to tears, Zuckerman called Essie in to keep
his mother company at breakfast and ran
downstairs after his brother. Henry seemed
so disturbed, so in need of consolation. But
when Zuckerman came out of the lobby onto
the sunny esplanade beside the pool, he saw
Henry already out on the street, making a
call in a phone booth. So, another love affair.
That torment too. *The Crisis,* thought Zuckerman, *in the Life of a Husband.*

In Miami Beach, Zuckerman had refrained
from bringing up the deathbed scene with his
brother. For one thing, their mother was
nearly always within earshot, and when he

and Henry were alone, either Henry was too unhappy to talk to or they were making plans for their mother's future. To their dismay, she had refused to come up with them to Jersey to stay awhile with Henry and Carol and the kids. Maybe later, but for now she insisted on remaining "close" to her husband. Essie was going to sleep on the living-room sofa bed so that their mother wouldn't be alone at night, and her canasta-club friends had volunteered to take turns staying with the grieving widow during the day. Zuckerman told Essie it might be wise if Flora Sobol was excused from duty. None of them was going to relish a piece in the *Miami Herald* entitled "I Sat Shiva with Carnovsky's Mother."

On the plane he had his first chance to learn what Henry thought about what he still couldn't puzzle out for himself. "Tell me something. What was Dad's last word that night? Did he say 'Better'?"

"'Better'? Could be. I thought he said 'Batter.'"

Zuckerman smiled. As in "Batter my heart, three-person'd God," or "Batter up!"? "You sure?"

"Sure? No. But I thought it was because of Essie talking about the old days and Grandma.

I thought he was all the way back, seeing Grandma over the mandel bread."

Well, there was Tolstoy, thought Zuckerman, to support Henry's conjecture. "To become a tiny boy, close to mother." What Tolstoy had written only days before his own death. "Mama, hold me, baby me..."

"I thought he said 'Bastard,'" Zuckerman told him.

Now Henry smiled. The smile his patients fell in love with. "No, I didn't hear that."

"I thought he might be writing one last letter to Lyndon Johnson."

"Oh, Christ," said Henry. "The letters," and went back unsmilingly to sipping his drink. Henry had received his share: after the near-defection at Cornell, a letter a week beginning "Dear Son."

Minutes later Henry said, "Even little Leslie, age seven, became a correspondent of Dad's, you know."

"I didn't."

"Poor kid. He's never gotten another, before or since. He thinks he should get mail all the time now, because of his three letters from Miami."

"What'd they say?"

"'Dear Grandson. Be nicer to your sisters.'"

"Well, from now on he can be as cruel to them as he likes. Now," Zuckerman added, remembering his brother dashing down to the outdoor phone booth, "we can all be as cruel as we like."

Zuckerman ordered a martini too. First time in his life he'd had a drink only an hour after his eggs. The same was certainly true for Henry. But the inner man was having his day.

Each finished the first drink and ordered a second.

"You know all I could think at the funeral?" Henry said. "How can he be in that box?"

"That's mostly what everybody thinks," Zuckerman assured him.

"The top is screwed on and he'll never get out."

They were flying over Carolina farmland. Clear from thirty-five thousand feet where Mondrian got the idea. The tons of tilled soil, the fibrous net of rooted vegetation, and his father under it all. Not only the lid, not only the few cubic feet of floury Florida loam and the dignified slab of marble to come, but the whole outer wrapping of this seven-sextillion-ton planet.

"Do you know why I married her?" Henry suddenly said.

Ah, so that's who's boxed in and will never get out. Dear Son. Screwed down beneath the tonnage of those two little words.

"Why?" asked Zuckerman.

Henry closed his eyes. "You won't believe this."

"I'll believe anything," Zuckerman told him. "Professional deformity."

"I don't want to believe it myself." He sounded sick with self-recrimination, as though he were sorry now that he'd planted a bomb in his luggage. He was unhinged, all over again. He shouldn't be drinking, Zuckerman thought. There would be worse recriminations later, if he went ahead and spilled some humiliating secret. But Zuckerman made no attempt to save his brother from himself. He had a powerful taste for such secrets. Professional deformity.

"Know why I married Carol?" This time he used her name, as though deliberately to make what he was about to confess more brutishly indiscreet. But it wasn't Henry's savagery, really; it was the savagery of his conscience, overtaking him before he'd even begun to violate its tenets.

"No," replied Zuckerman, to whom Carol had always seemed pretty but dull, "not really."

"It wasn't because she cried. It wasn't because she'd been pinned with the pin and then engaged with the ring. It wasn't even everybody's parents expecting us to...I loaned her a book. I loaned her a book, and knew if I didn't marry her I'd never see it again."

"What book?"

"*An Actor Prepares*. A book by Stanislavsky."

"Couldn't you buy another?"

"My notes were in it—from when I was rehearsing the Ragpicker. Do you remember when I was in that play?"

"Oh, I remember it."

"You remember that weekend I came home?"

"I sure do, Henry. Why didn't you go and ask her for the book?"

"It was in her room in the women's dorm. I thought of getting her best friend to steal it for me. This is true. I thought of breaking in there and stealing it myself. I just couldn't bring myself to say that I wanted it back. I didn't want her to know that we were about to break up. I didn't want her to think afterward that all I could think about at a time like that was my book."

"Why did you give it to her in the first place?"

"I was a kid, Nate. She was my 'girl.' I loaned it to her after our first date. For her to see my notes. I was showing off, I suppose. Oh, you know how you loan somebody a book. It's the most natural thing in the world. You get excited and you loan it to them. I was full of a friend I'd made—"

"Timmy."

"God, yes. Timmy. You remember. The Provincetown Players and Timmy. Not that I had an ounce of talent. I thought acting was seething and sobbing. No, nothing would have come of it. And it isn't that I don't love my own work. I do, and I'm goddamn good at it. But the book meant something to me. I wanted Carol to understand. 'Just read this,' I told her. And the next thing I knew, we were married."

"At least you got the book back."

He finished off the second drink. "And a lot of good it did me."

Then do him some good, thought Zuckerman. It's why he's made you his confessor. Help him raise this lid still holding him down.

Lend a hand. As their father used to say, "He's your brother—*treat* him like a brother."

"Did you ever act in Chekhov that year at Cornell?"

"I had a career of two plays at Cornell. Neither was Chekhov."

"Do you know what Chekhov said as a grown man about his youth? He said he'd had to squeeze the serf out of himself drop by drop. Maybe what you ought to start squeezing out of yourself is the obedient son."

No response. He had closed his eyes again—he might not even be listening.

"You're not a kid, Henry, beholden to narrow conventional people whose idea of life you're obliged to fulfill. He's dead, Henry. Aside from being in that box with the lid screwed down, he is also dead. You loved him and he loved you—but he tried to make you somebody who would never do anything or be anything that couldn't be written up in the *Jewish News* under your graduation picture. The Jewish slice of the American piety—it's what we both fed on for years. He'd come out of the slums, he'd lived with the roughnecks—it must have terrified him to think we'd grow up bums like Sidney. Cousin Sidney, collecting the quarters from the kids who sold the football pools. But to Daddy he was Longy Zwillman's right arm. To Dad he was Lepke."

"To Dad, becoming a drama major at Cornell made you Lepke." His eyes were still shut, and the smile was sardonic.

"Well, a little of Lepke wouldn't kill you at this point."

"It isn't me I'm worried about killing."

"Come on, you're a bigger character than this. An actor prepares. Well, you've been preparing for thirty-two years. Now deliver. You don't have to play the person you were cast as, not if it's what's driving you mad."

Inventing people. Benign enough when you were typing away in the quiet study, but was this his job in the unwritten world? If Henry could perform otherwise, wouldn't he have done so long ago? You shouldn't put such ideas in Henry's head, especially when he's already reeling. But reeling was when somebody could catch you right on the jaw. And besides, Zuckerman was by now a little drunk, as was his kid brother, and somehow a little drunk, it seemed to him idiotic that his kid brother shouldn't have what he wanted. To whom was he closer? Probably more corresponding genes in Henry than in any other animal in the species. More corresponding memories, too. Bedrooms, bathrooms, duties, diseases, remedies, refrigerators, taboos, toys, trips, teachers, neighbors, relatives, yards, stoops, stairwells, jokes, names, places, cars, girls, boys, bus lines...

Batter. The mixture time had beaten together for making Zuckermans. Suppose their father had closed things out with that: Boys, you are what I baked. Very different loaves, but God bless you both. There's room for all types.

Neither the Father of Virtue nor the Father of Vice, but the Father of Rational Pleasures and Reasonable Alternatives. Oh, that would have been very nice indeed. But the way it works, you get what you get and the rest you have to do yourself.

"How unhappy are you at home, Henry?"

He answered with his eyes pressed tightly shut. "It's murder."

"Then, for Christ's sake, start squeezing."

At Newark Airport Zuckerman's limousine was waiting. He had phoned early that morning from Miami to arrange to be met by a car with an armed driver. It was from the same outfit that drove Caesara around in New York. He'd found their card where he'd left it—his bookmark in Caesara's Kierkegaard. Before leaving for Miami, he'd pocketed the card, just in case. The book he still meant to return, but several times had restrained himself from sending it, in care of Castro, to Cuba.

He'd slept poorly the night before, thinking of his return to Manhattan and the possibility that the ravishing of his handkerchief by Pepler was not the end of his defilement but only the beginning. What if the wanton ex-Marine was packing a gun? What if he should be hiding in the elevator and try strangling Zuckerman to death? Zuckerman could not only envision the scene—by four a.m., he could smell it. Pepler weighed a ton and reeked of Aqua Velva. He was freshly shaved. For the murder or for the TV interview afterward? *You stole it, Nathan! My hang-up! My secret! My money! My fame!* JERK-OFF ARTIST KILLS BARD OF JERKING-OFF; ZUCKERMAN DEAD BY ONANIST'S HAND. Most disappointing to be gripped once again by such elemental fears—fears that by dawn had all but vanished; nonetheless, before leaving, he had phoned ahead to hire somebody at least to protect him during the initial

stage of reentry. But when he saw the limousine, he thought, *I should have taken the*
bus. Forget retribution. That's over too. There
are no avengers.

He walked up to the limousine. It was Caesara's young driver, in full livery and dark
glasses. "I'll bet you never thought you'd see
me again," said Zuckerman.

"Oh, yes I did."

He came back to his brother. Henry was
waiting to say goodbye before going to pick
his car up in the parking lot.

"I'm all alone," Zuckerman said. "If you
should need a place to sleep."

Henry recoiled a little at the suggestion.
"I have to get to work, Nathan."

"You'll call me if you need me?"

"I'm all right," Henry said.

He's angry, Zuckerman thought. Now he
has to go home knowing he doesn't have to.
I should have let him be. You can leave her
if you want to. Only he doesn't want to.

They shook hands in front of the terminal.
Nobody watching would ever have imagined
that once upon a time they had eaten ten
thousand meals together, or that only an hour
earlier they were momentarily as close as
they had been back before either had written

a book or touched a girl. A plane took off from Newark, roaring in Nathan's ears.

"He did say 'Bastard,' Nathan. He called you a bastard."

"What?"

Suddenly Henry was furious—and weeping. "You *are* a bastard. A heartless conscienceless bastard. What does loyalty mean to you? What does responsibility mean to you? What does self-denial mean, *restraint*— anything at all? To you everything is disposable! Everything is *ex*posable! Jewish morality, Jewish endurance, Jewish wisdom, Jewish families—everything is grist for your fun-machine. Even your shiksas go down the drain when they don't tickle your fancy anymore. Love, marriage, children, what the hell do you care? To you it's all fun and games. *But that isn't the way it is to the rest of us.* And the worst is how we protect you from knowing what you really are! And what you've done! You killed him, Nathan. Nobody will tell you—they're too frightened of you to say it. They think you're too famous to criticize—that you're far beyond the reach now of ordinary human beings. But you killed him, Nathan. With that book. *Of course* he said 'Bastard.' He'd seen it! He'd seen what you had done to him and Mother in that book!"

"How could he see? Henry, what are you talking about?"

But he knew, he knew, he knew, he'd known it all along. He'd known it when Essie, over their midnight snack, had told him, "If I were you, I wouldn't listen to one goddamn thing they say." He'd known during the rabbi's eulogy. And he'd known before that. He'd known when he was writing the book. But he'd written it anyway. Then, like a blessing, his father had the stroke that sent him into the nursing home, and by the time *Carnovsky* appeared he was too far gone to read it. Zuckerman thought he had beaten the risk. And beaten the rap. He hadn't.

"How could he see it, Henry?"

"Mr. Metz. Stupid, well-meaning Mr. Metz. Daddy made him bring it to him. Made him sit there and read it aloud. You don't believe me, do you? You can't believe that what you write about people has *real consequences*. To you this is probably funny too—your readers will die laughing when they hear this one! *But Dad didn't die laughing.* He died in misery. He died in the most terrible disappointment. It's one thing, God damn you, to entrust

275

your imagination to your instincts, it's another, Nathan, to entrust *your own family!* Poor Mother! Begging us all not to tell you! Our mother, taking the shit she's taking down there because of you—and smiling through it! And still protecting you from the truth of what you've done! You and your superiority! You and your hijinks! You and your 'liberating' book! Do you really think that conscience is a Jewish invention from which you are immune? Do you really think you can just go have a good time with the rest of the swingers without troubling yourself about conscience? Without troubling about anything but seeing how funny you can be about the people who have loved you most in the world? The origin of the universe! When all he was waiting to hear was 'I love you!' 'Dad, I love you'—that was all that was required! Oh, you miserable bastard, don't you tell me about fathers and sons! I *have* a son! I know what it is to love a son, and you don't, you selfish bastard, and you never will!"

Until the spring of 1941, when the boys were eight and four and the Zuckermans moved into the one-family brick house on the tree-lined street up the hill from the park, they had lived at the less desirable end of their Jewish neighborhood, in a small apartment building at the corner of Lyons and Leslie. The plumbing and the heating and the elevator and the drains were never working all at the same time, the Ukrainian superintendent's daughter was Thea the Tease, an older girl with a big bust and a bad reputation, and not everybody in the building had a kitchen floor like the Zuckermans' that you could eat off if worse came to worst. But because of the low rent, and because of the bus stop out front, it was an ideal place for the office of a young chiropodist. In those days Dr. Zuckerman's office was still in the front room where the family listened to the radio at night.

Across the street from the boys' back bedroom, on the other side of a high wire fence, was a Catholic orphanage with a small truck farm where the orphans worked when they weren't being taught—and, as Nathan and his little friends understood it, being beaten with a stick—by the priests in the Catholic school. Two old dray horses also worked on the farm, a most unexpected sight in their neighborhood; but then the sight of a priest buying a pack of Luckies in the candy store

277

downstairs, or driving by in a Buick with the radio on, was more unexpected still. What he knew about horses he knew from *Black Beauty;* about priests and nuns he knew even less—only that they hated the Jews. One of Zuckerman's first short stories, written in his freshman year of high school and called "Orphans," was about a small Jewish boy with a bedroom window overlooking a Catholic orphanage, who wonders what it would be like to live behind their fence rather than his. Once a dark heavyset nun had come over from the orphanage to have his father cut away an ingrown toenail. After she left, Nathan had waited (in vain) for his mother to go into his father's office with a pail and a rag to clean the door handles the nun had touched coming and going. He had never been more curious about anything in his life than about the nun's unshod feet, but his father said nothing that evening within hearing distance of the children, and at six, Nathan was neither young enough nor old enough to go ahead and ask what they looked like. Seven years later the nun's visit became the centerpiece of "Orphans," a short-short story sent out to the editors of *Liberty,* then *Collier's,* then *The Saturday Evening Post,* under the ersatz
278

name Nicholas Zack, and for which he received his first set of rejection slips.

Instead of going directly back to New York, he instructed the driver to follow the sign that said "Newark," postponing for just a while longer the life of the Nathan Zuckerman whom the mute inglorious little Zack had rather surprisingly become. He guided him along the highway and up the ramp to Frelinghuysen Avenue; then past the park and the tip of the lake where he and Henry had learned to ice-skate, and up the long Lyons Avenue hill; past the hospital where he had been born and circumcised, and on toward that fence that had been his first subject. His driver was armed. The only way, according to Pepler, to enter this city anymore.

Zuckerman pushed the button that lowered the glass partition. "What sort of weapon do you carry?" he asked the driver.

"A .38, sir."

"Where do you carry it?"

He slapped his right hip. "Like to see it, Mr. Z.?"

Yes, he should see it. Seeing is believing and believing is knowing and knowing beats unknowing and the unknown.

"Yes."

The driver hiked up his jacket and unsnapped a holster hooked to his belt, a holster not much larger than an eyeglass case. When they stopped for a light, he held up in his right hand a tiny handgun with a snub black barrel.

What is Art? thought Zuckerman.

"Anybody comes within ten feet of this baby is in for a big surprise."

The pistol smelled of oil. "Freshly cleaned," said Zuckerman.

"Yes, sir."

"Freshly fired?"

"On the range, sir, last night."

"You can put it away now."

Predictably the two-story apartment building where he'd first lived struck him as a lilliputian replica of the red-brick canopied fortress he'd have described from memory. Had there been a canopy? If so, it was gone. The building's front door was also gone, torn from its hinges, and, to either side of the missing door, the large windows looking into the foyer had lost their glass and were boarded over. There was exposed wiring where once there had been two lamps to light your way in, and the entryway itself was unswept and littered with trash. The building had become a slum.

Across the street, the tailor shop had become a store for idol worshippers—holy statuary on display in the window, along with other "Spiritual Supplies." The corner storefront, once a grocery, was now owned and occupied by the Calvary Evangelistic Assembly, Inc. Four stout black women with shopping bags were standing and talking at the bus stop. In his early childhood, four black women at the bus stop would have been domestics up from Springfield Avenue to clean for the Jewish women in the Weequahic neighborhood. Now they left the neighborhood, where they themselves lived, to clean for the Jewish women in the suburbs. Except for the elderly trapped in nearby housing projects, the Jews had all vanished. So had almost everyone white, including the Catholic orphans. The orphanage appeared to have been converted into some sort of city school, and there was a small new nondescript building on the corner where the truck farm had been. A bank. Looking around, he wondered who banked there. But for candles, incense, and holy statuary, nothing seemed to be for sale any longer on Lyons Avenue. There didn't seem to be anywhere to buy a loaf of bread or a pound of meat or a pint of ice cream or a bottle of aspirin, let alone a dress or a watch or a chair. Their little thoroughfare of shops and shop-keepers was dead.

Just what he wanted to see. "Over," he thought. All his lyrical feeling for the neighborhood had gone into *Carnovsky*. It had to—there was no other place for it. "Over. Over. Over. Over. Over. I've served my time."

He had the driver cruise slowly down the block toward Chancellor Avenue, the way he'd walked each morning to school. "Stop," he said, and looked up an alleyway between two houses to the garage where the super-intendent's wayward daughter, Thea, and the grocer's daughter, Doris, had enticed him one day by telling him how pretty he was. 1939? 1940? When they shut the garage doors he feared the worst—his mother had warned him that Thea was too "developed" for her age, and no one had to remind him that she was Christian. But all Thea made him do was stand beside a big black grease spot and repeat everything she said. The words meant little to him but a great deal obviously to Thea and the grocer's daughter, who couldn't stop giggling and hugging each other. It was his first strong experience of the power of language and of the power of girls; as the orphanage fence beyond his bedroom window was the first momentous encounter with caste and chance, with the mystery of a destiny.

A young black man, his head completely shaved, stepped out of one of the houses with a German shepherd and stared down from the stoop at the chauffeur-driven limousine in front of his alleyway, and at the white man in the back seat who was looking his place up and down. A chain fence surrounded the three-story house and the little garden of weeds out front. Had the fellow cared to ask, Zuckerman could without any trouble have told him the names of the three families who lived in the flats on each floor before World War II. But that wasn't what this black man wished to know. "Who you supposed to be?" he said.

"No one," replied Zuckerman, and that was the end of that. You are no longer any man's son, you are no longer some good woman's husband, you are no longer your brother's brother, and you don't come from anywhere anymore, either. They skipped the grade school and the playground and the hot-dog joint and headed back to New York, passing on the way out to the Parkway the synagogue where he'd taken Hebrew lessons after school until he was thirteen. It was now an African Methodist Episcopal Church.

ABOUT THE AUTHOR

Philip Roth was born in New Jersey in 1933. He studied literature at Bucknell University and the University of Chicago. His first book, *Goodbye, Columbus,* won the National Book Award for Fiction in 1960. He has lived in Rome, London, Chicago, New York City, Princeton, and New England. Since 1955, he has been on the faculties of the University of Chicago, Princeton University, and the University of Pennsylvania, where he is now Adjunct Professor of English. He is also General Editor of the Penguin Books series "Writers from the Other Europe." Recently he has been spending half of each year in Europe, traveling and writing.